MISSION OF LOVE

(Branyrd the Angel Series Book 3)

J.E. SPINA

PUBLISHED BY J.E. SPINA

COPYRIGHT 2023
J.E. Spina
Londonderry, New Hampshire

COVER BY JOHN SPINA

ALL RIGHTS RESERVED

ISBN (paperback) 979-8-9874646-2-5

Library of Congress Control Number: 2023917765

share this book with another person, please purchase an additional copy for each recipient.

Thank you for respecting the hard work of this author.

This book is a work of fiction. Any references to persons, places or things are purely coincidental. Names, characters, places, and events are products of this author's imagination.

ACKNOWLEDGEMENTS

A very special thank you to my incomparable beta readers, Patricia Bradley, Michelle Clement James, Michele Rolfe, John Spina and Frances Stewart for working tirelessly to read and review my work and for their helpful input. Their assistance is invaluable and appreciated.

Thank you to my husband, John, for the beautiful cover and for all the dinners he cooked that made it possible for me to continue to write.

DEDICATION

A special dedication to a long-time friend, Martin McGowan, who was an Angel to me and to many others whose lives he touched. He was taken from us in September of 2023. He will be greatly missed.

To all who believe in Angels around us – I think at the conclusion of this book those nonbelievers may become believers too.

Table of Contents

PREFACE

There are things in this book that cannot be explained to younger children making this is suitable for ages 17+. We all make mistakes but it is how we turn our lives around to correct them that matters. That is what Branyrd must do not only for herself but also for others.

This is the third book in the series. There will be another book coming, possibly more. Each book is a stand-alone story dealing in a new mission for the main protagonist. This genre is different from what I have written in the past. I wanted to combine good and evil in a new way through the eyes of an Angel named Branyrd. If you noticed, I capitalize the word Angel everywhere in order to make it stand out.

Some may believe in Angels on Earth while others are naysayers. I, for one, believe there is something greater than we are out there that is helping us along our troubled paths and trying to steer us in the right direction. We all need help at one time or another in our lives. Some of you may have somehow had your lives touched by an Angel as I have.

I think you just may change your mind about believing after reading about this Angel. I hope this story about Branyrd lightens your hearts, lifts your spirits, and brings a little joy your way.

I wrote this story for all those who are suffering during war time and to let them know that HE is watching over them and sending help in the form of an Angel.

PROLOGUE

The bombs were landing now in all parts of the small island that was once peaceful. There was nowhere to go. The inhabitants of some of the bombed buildings were trapped and screams of agony could be heard. One man went into a destroyed building where he lived and dragged out his family, his wife, two children and their dog. They were all knocked unconscious but alive with cuts and scrapes that would eventually heal.

He raised his hands toward Heaven and prayed with all his might as tears flowed freely across his dusty face leaving tracks. "Please, LORD, send us some help. We are desperately in need of your intercession. Thank you for sparing my family, dear LORD. But so many others have died or are going to die. I cannot save them in time. I am only one man. Please hear my prayers!"

***

The LORD sighed as HE watched this tragic scene play out. HE turned to Benedicto and said, "This is a job for you and Branyrd. Do you think she can handle this?"

"Yes, LORD. I am sure she can. She has become a force of her own as an Angel First Class. If she keeps this up, she may surpass all others at that level soon."

"Yes, I agree, Benedicto. I have seen much growth, strength, courage, and conviction during her last two missions. She will still need you close by to aid her in troubled times. This will be her most dangerous and trying mission of all."

"I will be there, LORD, and do all I can to assist her in any way YOU direct." Benedicto bowed and flew to the cloud where he would meet Branyrd as soon as she was told by HIM of this new Mission of Love.

CHAPTER ONE

Branyrd was getting restless and searched Heaven for a sign that it was time once again for her to be given another mission. She had grown exponentially during the other two missions and had met and made some special friendships that she would always treasure in her mind and hold close to her heart. She was not human but Branyrd felt that she did have a mind and a heart much like a human especially when she was on Earth. She had learned their ways, some negative, others positive, and knew what was expected of her while she was there.

The Angel had missed the smell and feel of the Earth and the smiles of her friends there. She thought fondly of all of them but knew that she would never see them again. She prayed that they would always remember her and hold her close to their hearts as she did with memories of them.

As Branyrd was daydreaming about her past missions she felt HIS presence all around her warming and lifting her up from her dream state. She looked up and smiled into HIS brilliant face that shone brighter than any light possible. She nodded to HIM as HE put out HIS hands to lift her up to stand before HIM.

Branyrd's wings spread out around her and glistened in HIS presence while her hair was bright and yellow as the sun as it cascaded down her back. Branyrd was a sight to behold but much larger in Heaven than her Earthly form would be. The LORD changed her form to blend in with those on Earth so as not to frighten them. Benedicto's form, however, was much larger than hers and stayed quite large when he was on Earth to protect Branyrd from any dangers that may come their way. It was the LORD's way of ensuring that Branyrd would always be safe from harm.

"It is time, Angel, for you to leave once again. Are you ready for another mission?"

"Oh yes, LORD. I am ready, more than ready. Ask me what YOU must, LORD," Branyrd said in a breathless whisper only HE could hear.

"There are many who are suffering on Earth. I have watched sadly what is happening there. There is war and many of MY people are suffering. I need you to help the children there in the war-torn areas to escape to safety and be nurtured back to good health. I will take care of the others and add them here to MY flock."

"How will you stop the war, LORD? Will YOU smite them? Branyrd asked in fear. She couldn't imagine what would happen to the people at war. She only hoped she could save some of them along with the children, but HE only said to save the young ones.

"Get yourself ready, Angel. Don't worry about anyone but the children right now. Guardian Angel Benedicto is waiting for you. He will guide you on your way and be there if you need him. Also, I am always here for you too, just a prayer away."

Branyrd bowed to HIM and flew over to the largest cloud where her Guardian Angel Most High was waiting with a broad smile and a wave beckoning her forward. Benedicto gripped her hands and they took off faster than Branyrd ever remembered before. She held her breath and gripped Benedicto's hands tighter.

"You did it again, Benedicto! You managed to frighten me half to death! I didn't think you could go any faster than last time but you somehow managed to do just that," Branyrd took a deep breath and sighed.

"No worries, Angel, we are here. Look around you and be careful where you walk. There is devastation everywhere."

The Angel opened her eyes and gasped at what she saw. There was smoke and dust rising from the ground making it difficult to see but as the dust cleared somewhat, she could see that all the buildings had been flattened. The only things still standing were iron rods that once held some of the buildings in place at one time, but even they swayed precariously back and forth in the smoke and dust. No vegetation or living things could be seen anywhere.

Branyrd sighed heavily as tears poured from her eyes. Now that she was on Earth, she felt human again with emotions and feelings that Angels do not have. She wiped her tear-soaked face with her sleeve and noticed that her clothes were camouflaged to blend into the surroundings. Benedicto wore similar clothes but of course his were a lot larger to fit his huge frame. The air around them was quite warm and she was relieved to be wearing shorts, a T-shirt and sturdy sneakers.

"Come, Angel. We mustn't dally here too long. There is danger at every corner of this damaged island. HE has instructed me to take you to the children's hospital and adjoining orphanage or what is left of these buildings. They have been heavily bombed too, unfortunately. You are needed there to help the children and get them to safety."

"Where do I take them, Benedicto?" Branyrd queried with a furrowed brow. Unfortunately, Benedicto was already way ahead of her. She had to hurry to catch up.

"You didn't answer me, Benedicto. Where do we go with the children if there is danger at every corner of the island?"

"HE will tell us soon, Angel. Be patient. Let's go see what the children need to prepare them for the trip."

CHAPTER TWO

Both the Candle Island Hospital and Sisters of Love Orphanage were gutted and nearly destroyed except for a small wing to the back of the hospital building. This is where Branyrd and Benedicto found at least two dozen children with some adults tending to them. A few of the adults were nuns who ran the orphanage. These people looked up when they saw two figures coming their way.

One nun, Sister Superior, came forward to greet them. "Who are you? Where did you come from? How did you get here?" she asked in confusion. Her questions rang through the air as the sister appeared startled by their sudden appearance.

Branyrd stepped forward and took Sister Superior's hand and blessed her. She said, "I am Branyrd. I have been sent to help you with the children. I can take them out of here to somewhere safe."

"Did HE send you?" Sister Superior asked as she watched Branyrd's face light up.

"Yes, HE did, Sister." Beckoning to her Guardian Angel she introduced him, "This is Benedicto. He is here to aid me in getting all of you out of here safely."

Sister Superior called over to her fellow nuns and told them what Branyrd had just said. She whispered, "She is an Angel. Who else would the LORD send to help us. She is no mortal person and must have powers to find us a haven for the children."

The other nuns agreed, bowed their heads, and blessed themselves as they looked at Branyrd and Benedicto.

"Let's gather up the children right away before more bombs come this way," Sister Superior directed the sisters.

Branyrd came closer to the sisters and thanked them. "I will need all of you to help me do this. It won't be easy to take all these children out of here. Are there any others in the buildings?"

"Yes, a few new mothers are here too with their infants. I sent them to the other side of the hospital building to find medical supplies in the infirmary. It is still partially standing. Thank God there were not many in the hospital besides the new mothers at the time of the bombing. The mothers and their newborns are all well."

"That is good news, Sister. Thank you," Branyrd said.

A few whimpers and groans were heard as a family, along with a limping dog, came into the building. "We need your help, Sisters," one man announced as he carried his young son. His wife followed closely behind, holding onto the hand of their daughter.

When the man spotted Branyrd, he exclaimed and dropped to his knees, "You have come! HE has sent you! You have come to help us! Bless the good LORD, bless you! I have prayed and you are here! Thank you, LORD!"

Branyrd removed the young boy out of the father's hands and looked him over for any injuries. "I am here to help you. Yes, HE has sent me. Are you all okay?" she directed her question to the parents as she took the little girl's hand and checked her also for any serious problems.

Branyrd said a silent prayer as she noticed some cuts and bruises on the children but some more serious ones on the parents. She ran her hands over the heads of the mother and then the father to ease their pain and help heal their cuts and internal bruising with the LORD's help.

The little boy announced in a relieved voice, "I feel better already. Did you make me all better, beautiful lady?" he asked as he looked up in awe at Branyrd whose head of golden hair was showing a brilliant light behind it.

"Are you an Angel?" the little girl asked as she watched Branyrd closely.

"I am the LORD's helper. HE has sent me to take you away from here to safety. Are you ready to go?"

"Yes, but I think you are really an Angel not just a helper," the little boy stated as he smiled at Branyrd. "Look at the light around your head! It is beautiful!"

His sister nodded in agreement and took his hand, holding onto it protectively and said, "We are ready to go with you,

Angel. Wherever you want to take us, right, Mommy and Daddy?"

The man gathered his family together and picked up the injured dog as he said, "Yes, we are ready to leave."

Branyrd put her hand over the head of the dog and prayed silently. The dog's head perked up; he licked Branyrd's hand, wagged his tail as his pain disappeared and wiggled to get out of his master's arms.

"Did you fix my dog too, Angel?" the little boy asked.

"Yes, HE helped to make your dog feel better so he could walk by himself."

"Who is HE?" the little boy asked.

"HE is our LORD. HE watches over all of us and helps us along our way in this life."

"Can I see HIM so I can thank HIM for fixing Misty?"

"No, you cannot see HIM here but if you say thank you, HE will hear you." Branyrd pointed up to the sky.

"Okay," the little boy said as he looked up to the sky and yelled, "Thank you, LORD, for fixing my dog and for making me and my family feel better."

Branyrd smiled and nodded, "I think HE heard you."

The little boy smiled back at the Angel and asked, "What is your name? My name is Seth. My sister's name is Freya."

"Nice to meet you, Seth and Freya. I am Branyrd and this is Benedicto. He is here to help me take care of all of you."

Seth opened his eyes wide with wonder when he spotted the huge man who stepped forward. "Wow, you are really big!"

"Yes, I am larger than you, that's for sure. Nice to meet you, Seth and Freya."

Seth asked, "Can I get a piggy-back ride on your back, Benedicto? I think you could carry almost all of us at once."

"Well, maybe I could," Benedicto laughed at the little boy's humor. "Do you want to hop on now? I can bend down and help you up."

"Oh yes, please! It will be so much fun!" Seth announced as he giggled in delight.

Benedicto bent down and helped Seth up onto his back and extended his hand to Freya to join her brother there.

Freya laughed and hopped up to hold on tight to her brother as they both held fast to Benedicto's neck.

There were smiles all around as the other children who were now in lines next to the nuns laughed, and one boy said, "We want to take turns next!"

"Okay, we can do that. We must hurry along now though," Branyrd instructed as she nodded to her Guardian Angel.

The Angel looked up and spotted a few planes circling overhead. She pulled the children closer in a circle around her and Benedicto and told the adults, "You must gather as close as you can to us so that you will be safe."

A few bombs began to land all around them, but did not touch or injure any of them for they were held protectively in the circle by the Angels.

Sister Superior blessed herself and began to pray along with her fellow sisters as each bomb struck closer and closer to them.

CHAPTER THREE

Bombs continued to drop as the group, tightly held together by Branyrd and Benedicto, moved as quickly as they could over the rubble that surrounded them. They picked their way carefully as more dust and debris fell in all directions.

Branyrd prayed silently too and kept looking up as still more bombs dropped from the skies. She was feeling the heat of the fires that were nearby and hoped that the children were not. She waved her hands around her as she prayed for the fires to stay away from them.

Benedicto spoke to Branyrd in her head and said, "I will lead the way, Angel. Follow me. HE has instructed that we go this way. HE has provided a place untouched by the bombs where we can rest the children for a while."

Each burned-out building the group passed left Branyrd with a deep anguish for she could hear the souls in there struggling to stay alive but with no hope of getting out. She prayed that HE would take them quickly and ease their suffering since she could not get over there to free them. She had a job to do and her job was to get the children out safely.

She struggled as she moved away and longed to do something to help them. HE spoke to her mind and told her, "I am taking care of them, Angel. You do not have to worry. They have already arrived and are sitting by MY side. They are in paradise and free of pain. Continue your way. There is much yet to be done."

"Yes, LORD. I will do all I can to follow YOUR instructions. But it is so difficult to ignore the anguish that I hear and feel deep inside me. It is torture."

"Relax and take a deep breath of the fresh air that I will keep around all of you. Hurry on your way and wait for MY instructions."

Branyrd nodded and sighed but took a deep breath as HE had instructed her. The children looked at the Angel when they heard her loud sigh. She smiled at them and patted them on their heads to ease their worries.

Benedicto raised his eyebrows in that funny way at Branyrd and spoke to her in her mind, "Do not worry, Angel. We are almost at the place where we can rest the children. You have to trust that HE will get us out of here."

"I know, Benedicto, but it hurts so much to hear and feel the pain of those that are suffering all around us."

The Guardian Angel stopped and looked ahead. There was a building still standing as HE had told them. The two Angels moved the children forward along with the sisters and new mothers in the rear with their babies held tightly against their chests in cocoons. Misty stayed by Benedicto's side keeping a close eye on Seth and Freya.

Branyrd smiled at the group and led the way into the large building that must have once been an office or some type of business with several floors. She kept the group together and instructed them, "We must stay here close to the exits in case we have to leave. There are bound to be more bombs soon."

"Are we going to die, Branyrd?" Seth asked in a tremulous voice as he jumped off Benedicto's back along with his sister.

"No, Seth. We will watch over you and keep you safe. HE doesn't want you to feel frightened. HE is watching over all of us."

"Should I thank HIM again, Branyrd?" Seth asked with wide eyes that were evidence of his anxiety.

"Sure, you can keep thanking HIM all you want. HE never gets tired of that. HE loves to hear from everyone."

Seth whispered to his sister, Freya, "We can thank HIM together. Okay?"

"You can also pray to HIM. HE loves to hear prayers," Branyrd stated with a beatific smile that lit up the room.

Suddenly a rumbling sound was heard nearby that continued to grow in intensity. The children all huddled together with the sisters and the mothers and babies as they all began to pray.

Branyrd led them in prayers as the sounds got closer and the building started to sway and shake; ceiling tiles began raining down on them. Benedicto and Branyrd raised their hands up to protect the group from injury.

Seth and Freya began to pray louder as some of the children cried and screamed in fright.

Branyrd whispered, causing them to calm down in order to hear what she was saying. "It's okay, children, do not fret. HE is watching over us. Listen, it is quiet once again. The bombs have stopped. You are safe."

Sighs of relief were heard as everyone cheered. "Hurray! See, our praying worked," Seth announced.

"I think it did, Seth," Branyrd smiled at him as he hugged her tightly.

"You shouldn't hug an Angel, Seth," Freya announced, not sure if that was allowed.

"No problem, Seth and Freya. I love hugs and give big ones back," Branyrd chuckled.

"See, Freya. It's okay to hug an Angel. In fact, Angels smell really nice and are soft like a fluffy cloud or my pillow."

Benedicto laughed out loud at that statement as he winked at Branyrd.

"What? Soft like a pillow?" Branyrd remarked silently, as she exchanged a furrowed brow at her Guardian Angel.

"Children always tell the truth, Angel," Benedicto retorted with a smirk.

The sisters gathered the children together and told them to lay down to rest until the Angels told them they could leave there.

Branyrd nodded to the sisters, "Thank you, Sisters, for doing that. The children do need to rest so we can move on to the next place that HE sends us."

Branyrd looked out a window at the devastation all around them. Everything was smoking and raising dust particles and debris into the air. It was not safe to go out there yet.

She whispered to Benedicto, "What are we going to do now? Once the children are rested enough, we need to keep moving."

"Yes, I agree, Angel, but HE has not sent further instructions yet. Only HE knows where it is safe to move them. By the appearance of things outside everything around us is gone. It won't be long before they flatten this building too. HE is holding it together for us for now."

"Why are they bombing this island? What is it called?"

"It is known as Candle Island since it is shaped like a candle. It was once part of the other islands that border it. They are known as the Peeples Islands. Candle Island got separated when the natives who live here decided that they wanted to return to the old ways and didn't need to be part of the Peeples Islands anymore. They are constantly at odds with one another over food, medicine, boundaries, and rules since they have separated. The group of the Peeples islands will not let inhabitants of Candle Island onto their island to work as they always have in the past. They do not want to share their wealth or their economy with traitors. That is what they call the Candlerians."

I don't understand how it helps anyone by bombing this little island," Branyrd stated, with a heavy heart.

"Men will always find a need to fight for something. It does sound meaningless to us. We don't live amongst them and their ways. They feel compelled to hold onto what is theirs or lose it forever."

"But all they are doing is destroying everything in sight, including innocent people. There will be nothing left to claim," Branyrd cried, as tears brimmed in her eyes.

"Yes, it is too sad to try to comprehend," Benedicto responded.

"How can we stop them from fighting one another?" the Angel inquired.

"I don't think it is our job to do that, Branyrd. HE will tell us what HE wants us to do. I don't think that will be one of the requests though."

"Can't these people just live in peace together and save so many lives that way? Who is going to live here with nothing left?" Branyrd asked in exasperation. "It just doesn't make any sense."

"Yes, I agree. It is an ongoing battle. Neither side will give in. Recently some Candlerians went across the borders of the other islands to steal some medicines that they cannot get on their own island and were arrested. Of course, this island wants their citizens back but have been refused unless they agree to the terms that the Peeples Islands lay out."

"What are the terms?" Branyrd asked, curiously.

"Well, Peeples Islands want to tax them higher for everything that is purchased and brought across from the other islands. They also expect to control the seas that border around the islands and put tariffs on everything. They are much richer and larger than the smaller Candle Island. It is not possible for these poor Candlerians to survive like this. That is why the group of islands began to bomb when the Candlerians refused to obey."

"What can we do to help these people, Benedicto?"

"I don't know. It is something that they have to work out themselves. All we can do is what HE has requested we do."

"I don't believe that HE sent us here to just rescue some children. There must be something else HE has in mind, Benedicto," Branyrd stated with a frown.

"That isn't a good look for you, Angel."

"What?"

"Your frown changes your angelic face so much that I don't know who you are," Benedicto laughed as he saw the Angel's frown deepen.

"Oh, never mind! You can be so exasperating at times, Benedicto!" Branyrd sighed and turned away from him and concentrated on the sleeping children who looked so peaceful in this time of chaos.

There had to be something that she could do to help this little island. Her mission would not be complete until she did whatever was needed to be done even if it was above and beyond what HE expected her to do.

CHAPTER FOUR

There was a shuffling of feet heard outside the door near where Branyrd was sitting. She looked outside and spotted several soldiers with guns moving about.

"Benedicto, there are armed soldiers outside. They are heading this way. We must protect the children and the others."

The Guardian Angel looked out and whispered, "Get the children to the back of the building into a room and close and lock the door."

"What are you going to do, Benedicto?"

"Let me see if I can get them to go away. Hurry now and get the children out of harm's way."

"Okay." Branyrd moved quickly to rouse the children and adults and move them to safety. She stepped out of the room and joined Benedicto at the door.

"No, Angel. You must go back there too," he urged.

"I will not abandon you. It is my mission, after all, remember." Branyrd gave him her meanest frown yet.

He smirked and raised his eyebrow back at her.

She stifled a giggle even in these times of stress but put on a serious face to meet the soldiers.

Benedicto filled the doorway with his huge and powerful body as he met the men face to face.

The men backed away in terror when they spotted this giant of a man. One man ventured to step forward. "Who are you? What are you doing here on our island? You do not look like you are from around here."

"No, I am not from this part of the world. I am here to help my ..." Before Benedicto could come up with a reason for being there, Branyrd stuck her head out beside him.

"I am his sister. He came to get me. I was visiting some friends at the orphanage and got stuck here when the bombing began. We need to get to safety." Branyrd crossed her fingers and whispered up to the LORD, "Sorry about that."

The men whispered to each other and then smiled. "Do you know Sister Superior?"

"Yes," Branyrd improvised, waiting for the man to respond.

"I see. She is a friend of my mother's. She is a kind lady. We just came from the orphanage and did not find her or any of the children. Do you have them with you here?"

"Well, we…," Branyrd began but was afraid to answer this.

"Do not fear us. We are Candlerians and here to rescue the children and the sisters. We wanted to get them out of the village to the outskirts where there is no fighting or bombing going on. Others have already escaped there."

"I see. Yes, we do have them all here. Can you make sure that they will be safe from harm?" Branyrd asked, unsure whether she should trust the soldiers.

"Of course. We do not harm our own. We are not just soldiers but also men who have families of our own and want to make sure the village is empty of citizens."

"Okay. Then I will get the children, sisters, and mothers to follow you if you know somewhere safe to go."

"Yes, we do. Are the children unharmed?"

"Yes, I checked them over and they are okay with minor cuts and scrapes that will heal," the Angel responded.

"Follow us," the soldier said as he relayed to his men what they were going to do.

The men nodded in agreement and waited for the children and others to come out of the building.

One child recognized his uncle and cried out, "Uncle Sal! You came to get me!"

"Yes, I did, Dack. Are you okay?" the soldier said as he bent down to hug the boy.

"I am fine, Uncle Sal. I am not afraid of the bombs. I have been very brave, haven't I, Angel?" he said as he turned to Branyrd.

"Angel? Who is an Angel?" his uncle asked in confusion.

"She is," Dack said as he pointed to Branyrd.

"Oh, I see. She rescued you and now you think she is an Angel," he said as he snickered to his fellow soldiers who laughed with him.

Branyrd smiled at the men who took notice of her blond hair that shone like it was on fire.

"What is wrong with your hair? Is it on fire?" one soldier exclaimed, in alarm.

"Oh no, of course not," Branyrd said with a smirk. "It is only the dust that is flying around making it look like that."

"Oh. Okay. We better be on our way now before there are any more bombs coming. We need to get to safety before dark."

Branyrd and Benedicto gathered the group outside and explained, "We are going to be escorted out of the village by these soldiers. They are Candlerians just like you are, so you are safe."

"Aren't you coming with us, Branyrd and Benedicto?" Freya asked with frightened eyes.

"Of course, we are, Freya. No need to be frightened. They will not harm any of us. I will make sure of that," Branyrd stated as she patted Freya on the back.

The soldiers smiled at the little girl and nodded. "We will not hurt you. We promise, but you must hurry along so we can get there before dark. It will be more difficult to move in the dark. We cannot use flashlights or alert the enemy where we are."

"Will they shoot at us if they see us?" Seth asked in a shaky voice.

"No worries. We will protect you. Now hurry along, children," the soldiers instructed in a patient and kindly manner.

Branyrd and Benedicto spoke to each other silently in their heads about what their next moves would be.

"How far are they taking us? Will it be safe where we are going?" Branyrd questioned.

"I believe that they are not dangerous and mean what they say about getting us to safety. They are being cautious by moving us along as quickly as they can. It would be more dangerous in the dark without knowing where we are stepping. We could step on a bomb."

"Step on a bomb!" Branyrd cried out in alarm.

"Yes, there are bombs that did not explode everywhere. It happens sometimes. They can explode though if you step on them unaware."

"We cannot let the children do that. I will tell the sisters and adults to be watchful," Branyrd stated as she went to the back and spoke with each adult.

Sister Superior blessed herself and instructed her sisters to be careful where they walked with the children.

One of the soldiers stayed at the back of the line and overheard what they were saying. "There is no need to worry, Sisters. You are safe. The men in the front are looking carefully where they walk and will guide all of us in the right direction without any problems."

"That's good to know. Thank you, soldier. We owe you our lives. We will say prayers for you and your men that you will get back home safely too after this war is over."

"Thank you, Sisters. We can use all the prayers we can get to survive this crazy war."

Branyrd went back to Benedicto and reported, "The soldier in the back assured us that we are safe if we follow the men in front. They will lead us safely.

"I am not worried in the least, Angel. Who do you think sent these men to us?"

"HE did, right?"

"Yes, of course, HE did. We will be okay once we get to the next place away from the bombing."

"Okay. I believe you and trust you implicitly, Benedicto. I just didn't know if I could trust these soldiers to bring us to safety."

"Relax, Angel. All will be well. HE will tell us if we are in danger and protect us."

"I hope so," Branyrd said as she watched the soldiers moving through a field now that was free of any signs of bombing.

"Look ahead, Branyrd. There's another village along the beach that is untouched by the bombs. We will be safe there for now until we are given more instructions."

"Okay, it does look promising. I am not as patient as you are, Benedicto. I must learn to be more so eventually."

"In time you will learn to be more patient, Angel. Don't worry," Benedicto said with a smirk.

Branyrd turned to thank the soldiers but they had disappeared into thin air.

CHAPTER FIVE

The little village appeared like an oasis once the tall grasses separated revealing a beautiful beach with palm trees swaying in the breeze and clean air free of smoke and debris. It was as if they had entered another realm away from the bombing, offered to them by HIM.

There were huts situated all along the beach with umbrellas out front made of palm branches with little tables under them. Once the group spotted these umbrellas the children ran over, sat under them, and lay down in the sand. People came out of the huts to greet the visitors and welcome them to their huts for refreshments. The islanders fussed and fretted over the children to make sure they were not hurt, bandaged their small cuts, and gave them some pineapple juice and jerk chicken on sticks to eat.

The sisters and mothers with their new infants joined in and were given a basin of water to wash and then ushered to chairs that suddenly appeared on the sand. The mothers fed their babies while they sipped the juice and ate the chicken that was offered.

Branyrd and Benedicto watched in awe as everyone appeared relaxed and relieved to be safe from the bombing which was a distant memory now.

"This is strange, Benedicto," Branyrd said with a furrowed brow. "It's as if the bombing never happened."

"I agree, Angel. But HE is watching over and giving us this little retreat for the time being. It could disappear."

"What? You mean that this could all be in our minds and not exist at all," Branyrd asked in disbelief.

"Yes. We will know soon though. Let's go talk to the natives in the huts and see what they have to say."

Branyrd followed Benedicto to the first hut closest to them and knocked and then entered. An old man and woman, sitting at a small table sipping their drinks, looked up as they entered.

"Are you with the children out there?" the old woman asked in a gravelly voice.

"Yes, we were all brought here by the Candlerian soldiers. We needed a place to keep the children safe from the bombing," Branyrd said with a smile.

"Candlerian soldiers?" the old couple exchanged confused looks.

"Well, you are all safe here for now. We have not been bombed yet and hope that it will stay that way," the old man stated as he met their eyes with a kind gaze. He continued, "You are all welcome to stay here for as long as necessary Others have come here before you to escape the bombing. All are welcome."

Branyrd smiled and said, "Thank you, kind sir. You are most generous. We have nowhere else to go right now. We are at your mercy until we know what is going to happen next."

"Where did you two come from? You are not natives from here or the other islands nearby," the old woman dared to ask, as she gazed up at the giant of a man standing in her kitchen towering over her.

Benedicto stepped forward to answer, "No, we are not from around these parts. We have come a long way to help the children. I am Benedicto and this is Branyrd."

"Nice to meet you both. We are Mortan and Miriam. Thank you both for saving our island children. We have not been able to leave here since the bombing began in the next village. The air, thank goodness, is clear here for now, thanks to the breezes that blow off the ocean pushing the smoke away from here. If the bombing continues or comes any closer to us it will not stay this way. We don't know what we will do then. There is nowhere else to go. We cannot go to the other islands where we are not welcome," Miriam said as she reached out her hand in gratitude to the Angels.

"It is our pleasure to meet you both," Branyrd said as she shook Miriam's hand and then Mortan's and Benedicto did the same.

"Yes, I heard about that. It is too sad to think about the fact that you cannot live in peace together," Branyrd stated in a melancholy tone.

"Yes, some people do not accept our ways. We only want to live in peace and be able to live our way as our ancestors have always done. What the ruler on the other islands wants to do is modernize our island even more than it already is. But what he doesn't realize is he has destroyed most of the buildings that he once built and will never be replaced by us," Mortan said with a deep sigh.

"Please come in and have some juice and meat," Miriam said with a wave of her hand.

"Thank you. We are not hungry but could use a wash if you have some water," Branyrd specified.

"Of course, please come this way," Miriam led Branyrd and Benedicto to the sink that held a bowl filled with water.

After they both washed their hands and faces, they returned to speak further with the old couple.

"What can we do to help you?" Branyrd asked.

"Help us?" Mortan asked in confusion.

"We don't need any help. But you do, don't you?" Miriam asked, amused.

"No, we are fine. But we can help you in any way that you need while we are here," Branyrd answered in a soft and calm voice.

"There is no need to do anything for us. If we are bombed, we are all lost. No one can help us," Mortan said, sadness etching deep wrinkles on his face.

No sooner after Mortan's words were delivered, incoming bombs could be heard going off nearby as planes flew over the beach.

Branyrd rushed out to check on the group who had been laying out on the sand, relaxed and slowly falling asleep.

They jumped up in alarm at the sounds and gathered tightly together once they spotted Branyrd and Benedicto coming their way.

"Are you all okay?" Branyrd asked as she got closer to them.

"Yes, we are all right, Branyrd. We are brave, right Freya?" Seth announced with bravado as Misty jumped up and down and barked at the planes.

Branyrd patted them both on their heads and chuckled.

The sisters and new mothers came forward and gathered around to also check on the children as Benedicto looked up to see if there were any more planes coming their way.

It quieted down and no more bombing could be heard which didn't leave anyone feeling much safer.

Branyrd sat down next to Seth and Freya and asked, "Did you get enough to eat and drink?"

Seth cuddled up next to Branyrd and smiled at her beautiful face, "Yup, I did! I love pineapple juice and jerk chicken. My mother always makes this kind of chicken for us but not as often as I want it."

"Yes, she does, Seth. You eat it all and leave nothing for me. I always get Mommy to make extra so Daddy and I can get some."

Seth giggled, "That's because you are too slow when you eat. I eat faster!"

Branyrd snickered and covered her mouth so Seth couldn't hear her. She looked over at the children's parents and smiled. They nodded in agreement with what their daughter had said.

Benedicto leaned down to whisper in Branyrd's ear. "We need to leave the beach now and get out of the open. The planes have spotted us and could come back this way."

"Okay," she whispered back to him and gathered the group together. "We need to go inside the huts or away from the open so that the planes can't see us."

"Will they come back and bomb us on the beach, Branyrd?" Seth asked in a frightened voice.

"I don't think so but we want to be away if they do come back, just in case."

"Okay," Seth grabbed his sister's hand and she in turn took the hand of another child until they formed a chain and followed behind the Angels as they were led off the beach and into the huts where the natives welcomed them all with open arms.

They closed the doors of the huts tucking the group safely inside just as a few planes flew overhead and dipped down to get a closer look at the area and then flew away.

CHAPTER SIX

"That was a close call, Benedicto!" Branyrd stated with a sigh of relief.

"No worries, Angel. HE is watching over us."

"Thank you, LORD!" Branyrd whispered as she looked up into the blue sky now dotted with clouds from the planes.

"Branyrd, can I ask you a question?" Seth whispered as he came closer to her.

"Of course, Seth. What is it?"

"Does HE know me?"

"Yes, HE knows all of us."

"HE does? How does HE know so many people?"

"Well, for one thing, Seth, HE is responsible for us being here. HE put us all here on Earth."

"HE did? Wow! That is awesome!" Seth gushed with a broad smile.

Freya frowned at her brother, "Of course HE did! That is what we learn in Sunday school. Well, you will be going there soon, little brother. You have a lot to learn. Except, we no longer have a school. It was bombed."

"He will learn all there is to know about the LORD at that time, Freya. But in the meantime, you could teach him what you know. That will help Seth understand it better. Don't worry about your school. We will help rebuild it."

"That's good. Thank you, Branyrd. Okay, I guess I could help Seth. I don't know if I know everything yet though. I may need someone to teach me more too."

"Well, your parents will teach you and I am also here if you need to ask any questions at all," Branyrd said with a smile.

Freya looked at the Angel and smiled back but then turned to her brother and said, "I will help you, Seth, if you want to learn about the LORD. Okay?"

"Okay, Freya. Thank you. Can you tell me if HE is going to keep us safe now? Will we die?"

"I…I don't know, Seth," Freya said in a frightened voice as her face turned white and she looked at Branyrd for help.

"Don't worry, Seth. HE is watching over us right this minute. HE is the one that brought us here safely."

"HE did?" Seth looked up to the sky and waved and said, "Thank you, LORD."

Their parents wrapped both children in their arms when they heard Seth's remark as they nodded to Branyrd.

Branyrd felt her heart swelling or at least what she thought was her heart as a human temporarily. Tears filled her eyes as she tried to cover them up by a quick swipe of her hand.

Her Guardian Angel, Benedicto, noticed this and patted her on the back as he whispered, "You are showing your human side again, Angel."

She nodded and gave him a nudge and a smirk as she looked back at the children who were under her care. She whispered to HIM, "LORD, I hope YOU will give me some idea what we are to do next, for I don't have a clue."

Seth and Freya's parents smiled at Branyrd and said, "I hope our children are not bothering you too much, Branyrd. They do tend to ask a lot of questions."

"Not at all. I enjoy answering any questions they have. That is how they learn about the LORD."

Before Branyrd could say another word, a thundering sound was heard as the children cried out in fear as Misty pressed into Seth and Freya for protection. They huddled close together in the hut and looked toward Branyrd for guidance.

Branyrd glanced at Benedicto and asked, "What was that? What's going on now? Should I go outside and look?"

"Not yet, Branyrd. I will look." Benedicto opened a window in the hut and stuck his head out a little to see what had caused that sound.

What he saw was a surprise. He quickly closed the window and took Branyrd aside. "There are boats out there with

45

many natives heading this way. One of the boats was bombed by a plane and is now in pieces."

"We should go out there to rescue them. They need our help."

"Wait here. I will see what I can do," Benedicto stated as he opened the door and walked out.

Branyrd watched from the window as several boats were pulling up onto the beach and natives were gathering on the sand. Some of the people were injured and laying down as others attended to their needs.

Benedicto walked up to the first boat and introduced himself, "I am Benedicto and sent here to help you."

"Where did you come from?" one native asked in awe of the Guardian Angel's massive size.

"I have come from a distant place to assist you." He bent down to look at the injured and waved his hands over them.

Seeing this, Branyrd came rushing out and did the same to the others who were bleeding from injuries with a prayer and assistance from HIM.

The natives watched as this small woman administered to their injured companions and waited to ask her who she was.

"Who are you?" one native asked as he was struck by the Angel's golden hair and the light that emanated from behind her.

Branyrd smiled and placed her hand on the native's arm to calm him as she answered, "I am Branyrd. I have come with Benedicto to help all of you in any way we can."

"Don't you know we are at war?" one man questioned in surprise.

"Yes, we know. We have come to rescue the children who were trapped inside the hospital and orphanage."

Hearing this the sisters and others came out of the huts and walked over to Branyrd staying behind her in solidarity.

Sister Superior spoke up first, "Everything that Branyrd said is true. She rescued all of us. We owe her our lives. She was sent from above."

"I see," the leader said as he stepped forward and reached out his hand to Branyrd and Benedicto.

He stated, "We appreciate you are here and welcome your help. We escaped our island nearby and had nowhere else to go. We spotted this beach and hoped to stay here away from the bombing. But then the plane came over and dropped a bomb onto our boat."

"It is safe here for now. Bring your injured to the huts and stay away from the beach. The planes have been searching for us," Benedicto said as he picked up two of the injured in one swoop.

The huts were filled now as the injured were helped while the two groups of natives got acquainted and joined together in peace. They discussed what was happening on their respective islands and couldn't understand why. The elderly couple translated all the dialects for the Angels.

"What are we supposed to do now? The planes will come back and we will all be killed," the leader of the visiting natives stated.

The old couple in the first hut listened to the man and asked, "Which Island do you come from? Is your island damaged too?"

"We are all part of this archipelago. We live on Peeples Island right next door. Your island is the only one that is somewhat separated by the ocean. The rest of the six islands are closer together. And yes, our island is also damaged, which is the reason why we left there. We don't understand why anyone wants to harm us. We must do something to stop them."

"The old couple agreed and shrugged. "What can we do? We are just a small island with few natives left. There are others that did not survive in the nearby village that was damaged."

The natives turned to the Angels and asked, "Can you help us? We are unable to do anything about protecting ourselves and our people alone."

"That is why we are here," Branyrd said as Benedicto nodded in agreement.

Branyrd didn't feel at all confident and had no idea what to do as she kept a calm façade and opened a channel to the LORD for help.

CHAPTER SEVEN

Seth and Freya's parents spoke up as they looked at the Angels, "We will do whatever we need to do to keep our children safe. What do you want us to do?"

"When we know what HE wants us to do, we will let you know," Branyrd stated as she kept her voice steady even as she felt shaky inside.

The Angel looked Heavenward and prayed for guidance as more bombs came down destroying the rest of the boats that were on the beach.

The natives looked on in horror as all their boats were demolished leaving only scraps of wood floating on the water's edge.

"What do we do now? There is no way to leave the island!" the leader cried out in alarm.

Benedicto went to inspect the damage and shook his head. "They are all gone. Come help me gather the wood so we can salvage it. We may be able to build another boat. We must work together."

Branyrd assisted the men and women to gather what they could use as the children looked for smaller pieces of wood to carry back onto the beach behind the huts. They laid all the pieces out and tried to put them together with palm branches as they worked as a team.

Benedicto did what he could to direct the men and added a little of his own expertise with HIS help to keep the pieces lined up so they would fit tight enough to keep the water out.

The children were told to search for the plants that had a glue-like substance inside their stems that could help with the building. The adults described the plants to the children and warned them not to open the plant stems or their fingers would become stuck to the plants.

Hearing this, Branyrd offered to help the children so there wouldn't be any problems with that happening.

Freya and Seth were excited to take part in this search and raced ahead of their parents and Branyrd checking all the plants as they went along. Misty was always close by to supervise what the children were doing.

The sisters kept some of the children together to keep an eye on them in case they wandered too far away. The sisters held a few baskets that Miriam had given them to collect the plants.

Branyrd prayed as she followed close behind Freya and Seth guiding them to the right plants. She offered to cut them so that the children would not get sticky fingers. HE helped Branyrd by separating the stems for her as she carefully picked them up and placed them into the baskets.

When they had the baskets full, they all returned to the huts and gave the plants to the natives to use to complete their project. Benedicto was there to make sure the sticky substance dried and held the wood together firmly.

Once all the pieces of wood were bound together with palm trees, leaves and glue the men pushed the boat to the water to see if it was sea worthy. Benedicto pushed it further into the water and jumped in to test it. The natives all held their breaths as the boat dipped precariously low, almost capsizing with the weight of the massive man who sat in it smiling and waving to them.

"It's safe, everyone! If I can sit in it then it is safe for many of you to sail away."

"It's not safe to be out in open water, though!" one native exclaimed as he looked up at the sky.

"They won't be coming now. I am sure of it. They already destroyed your boats."

"But…where are we going to go?" one woman asked in a shaky voice.

"Maybe you should go to one of the other islands to talk to them, see how you can settle your differences and tell them to stop the planes coming over."

"I don't know if they will listen to us. Will you come with us? Maybe when they see you, they will be more receptive to us. We need to see our ruler there on the mainland."

Benedicto contemplated this with HIM and then smiled, "I think I can do that. I will help you convince the other islands to listen to reason. Maybe they will change their minds and agree to stop the bombing."

"Great!" the leader of the natives gathered all the men he could fit into the boat along with Benedicto and they sailed away.

Branyrd watched in awe as Benedicto waved to her and spoke to her mind, "Don't worry, Angel. I will be back. We need to talk to the other islanders and try to convince them that they should try to get along and stop this war before too many more lose their lives. HE is with us and will help. Take care of the others until I return."

The Angel shook her head and took a deep breath. "I don't believe it!" she said in exasperation.

She looked up to Heaven and beseeched HIS help. "What are we going to do now, LORD? We need you to help us. Please keep Benedicto and the rest of the men safe."

Branyrd was deep in concentration with the LORD and didn't hear a little voice calling to her. "Branyrd, are you all right?"

Branyrd looked down and said, "Oh, sorry, Seth. I didn't hear you. I was praying to HIM."

"You were praying to the LORD for help?"

"Yes, I was. We all need HIS help."

"But what do you need help with and where did Benedicto go with the other men?"

The Angel sighed and answered, "Well, Benedicto went to help the men make peace with the other islands so they will stop bombing here. I was praying for Benedicto and the other men to be safe in their travels."

"Oh, does that mean there will not be any more war? Are we now safe?"

"I don't know that yet. HE hasn't told me. I must stay here to keep you safe until HE tells me what else to do."

Branyrd guided Seth back to the huts so she could speak with the natives about peace.

"I need to speak with the adults, Seth. Go play with the other children. I will talk to you again soon," Branyrd said as she patted the boy on the head as he passed by.

"I need to speak to all of you for a moment," Branyrd addressed the natives in their language who were inside one of the huts.

"What do you need, beautiful lady?" one native woman asked. "How do you know our language?"

"I am a quick learner and, HE helped me. Can we gather all the islanders together to discuss what we need to do?"

"Of course," she replied as she went from hut to hut and gathered all the natives on the beach in front of Branyrd.

Branyrd looked at all the natives' anxious faces as they waited to hear what she had to say.

CHAPTER EIGHT

Back on the other islands the natives and Benedicto carefully made their way to the ruler of the largest of the Peeples Islands. The natives there opened the doors to the large hut that housed the ruler and moved away as they watched in awe the huge man, who moved effortlessly as if he was floating on air, walk inside with the other natives.

The ruler, Kamalnayo, waved them forward and directed them to sit in front of him on pillows of palm leaves as he sat high upon his throne chair.

The natives were nervous as they looked around praying that they would not be struck down for being in the ruler's presence. They waited for Benedicto to explain why they were there.

Benedicto smiled benevolently at the ruler who became uneasy in the huge man's presence. There was something about this man who appeared more than just a man, carried himself with poise and ease despite his size, and spoke softly but clearly in the ruler's language, much to Kamalnayo's surprise.

At once Kamalnayo relaxed as he spoke quickly with the giant of a man, curious to ask him many questions of where he came from and why he was there. "I am Kamalnayo, ruler of the Peeples Islands. Why are you here?"

Benedicto introduced himself and explained, "I am Benedicto. We are here to ask that you stop the bombing of Candle Island and the Peeples Islands and begin to make peace for these people. They have suffered enough. Even some of these men I brought with me say that you are bombing this island too. They escaped to Candle Island."

"I see. The Peeples Islands were not supposed to be touched, only Candle Island. They promised me."

"Who promised you?" Benedicto queried.

"Never mind. Where do you come from and why do you want to help our islands make peace?"

The Guardian Angel stated with a serious expression that held the ruler transformed, afraid to move unless he missed one word from this man, "There are many people suffering, some dying or already dead from your bombs that keep coming over Candle Island. These natives need peace to recover their dead, heal their injured and bring their families back to their homes to rebuild what you have destroyed."

"I see, but you did not tell me where you come from and why you are interested in helping our islands come to peace."

"I have been sent by HIM from a place far from here to help you."

"HIM? Who is this HIM you talk about?" the ruler asked in confusion.

"Do you not worship your gods here? Do you not have one special deity?"

"Yes, we do. But who is HIM?"

"HE is the God of all deities. HE is the one who put you all here. HE is the one who gives you food, love, family, and an island to live on."

"No, that cannot be. Our gods have done all that. How can you prove this?"

"I cannot prove it but HE can." Benedicto raised his hands toward Heaven and prayed.

Kamalnayo watched and listened to the man's strange words that he could not understand.

"Who are you speaking to and what did you say?"

"I asked HIM to show you the way to peace."

"What way is that?"

"The way to be kind to your fellow islanders, show them love and care for them like they are your own family, because they are. You are all one big family."

Kamalnayo shook his head. "Only our gods can do that."

"Can your god do this?" Benedicto pulled a pineapple out of thin air and handed it to Kamalnayo.

The ruler gasped in surprise and took the pineapple to inspect it. "How did you do that?"

"I told you; I do not do things. Only HE can do this through me."

"But…" Kamalnayo shook his head and looked wide-eyed at Benedicto. "What else can HE do? Can HE put fresh water in our wells? Can HE heal my sick child who has a fever and does not eat? Can HE put babies into the wombs of our women who cannot bear children?"

"Yes, to all those things. But you must pray to HIM and ask HIM to help you and stop this war now."

"How do I know HE will do all this if I stop the war?"

"HE will know if you pray to HIM. All good things will come to you in time."

"I want my son healed now. Can you ask HIM to do that? If HE does this, I will believe in HIM, pray to HIM, and stop this war."

"I will confer with HIM now. Wait a moment," Benedicto said as he raised his hands to Heaven once again and prayed that HE would help.

Everyone watched transfixed as the huge man stared up to the skies, raised his large hands, and spoke in a strange tongue. The ruler spoke to a few of his men and requested, "Bring my son to me now. Lay him next to me here."

The men raced to the ruler's hut where his wife and family were and came back with the boy on a stretcher between two palm trees with many pillows.

The boy was white, thin, and barely breathing. The ruler touched his son's face and whispered to him, "Soon you will be well, my son. Keep breathing."

Benedicto looked down upon the boy's slack face and withered body as he placed his hands on the boy's head and heart. He looked up to Heaven and prayed.

There were gasps of disbelief as the boy moved slightly, first his hands and then his feet. He suddenly sat up and looked around. "Father, I am hungry!" he stated as everyone jumped up in celebration and were racing here and there to get food for the ruler's now-healed son.

Kamalnayo fell to his knees and cried as he held his son in his arms and didn't let go.

"Father, why are you crying? Please don't hold me so tight. You are hurting me."

"Oh, Hanomelo, you are well, my son! You are healed by HIM!"

"HIM? Who is that, Father?"

"See this man in front of you? It is his god who healed you. We must pray to HIM so that HE will help us with everything we need."

"Can I eat now, Father? I am really hungry! I feel as if I have not eaten in a long time."

"Yes, of course, my son. You must be starving. You haven't eaten in a very long time."

The ruler turned to Benedicto and put his hand out in thanks, "I didn't believe your god could do this. I have prayed to our gods but they did not listen to me. How come your god listened to you?"

"HE listens to all those who pray daily to HIM. You must do this every day. HE will not give you everything you ask for but only what HE thinks you will need. You must understand this. HE knew that you needed your son to be well. That is why HE healed him."

"Do you mean that HE may not think that I need water in our wells, or babies in the wombs of our women?"

"Yes, that is correct. But you should not stop praying to HIM since HE gave you back your son, the most precious of all to you."

"Yes, of course, my son is the most precious one to me. I am grateful to your god for this. I will pray."

"But you must not forget your promise to stop this war also."

"I will think about this." Kamalnayo closed his eyes and then said, "I have thought about it. I will do my best to stop the planes from coming to the Candle Island."

Benedicto stared at the ruler but did not smile or speak. He waited for Kamalnayo to say something else.

"I promise I will stop this war but it may not be easy since I did not send those planes. We do not have any planes or bombs to do this. They were sent from another island that wants to take over all the islands here. They promised not to attack my island here but just the smaller island, Candle Island, where not as many natives live. They promised me many things to help my people prosper if I let them do this. I feel sad to see this happening to my people but I have to do this in order to save the rest of us. I don't know what will happen next. I will still be ruler. We do not have any way to protect ourselves from such powers."

"You will speak to ruler of this island and do your best, Kamalnayo," Benedicto retorted with a frown. "Remember HE will be watching over you." The Guardian Angel backed away and walked out of the hut along with the other natives to return to their boat to go back to Candle Island.

Kamalnayo watched the giant leave with the natives following close behind and turned to his son who was stuffing himself with enough food to feed a few men.

The ruler sat with his son and drank some pineapple juice from the pineapple that the giant had given him. It was the sweetest juice he had ever tasted. He smiled and looked upward in thanks but soon frowned with worry about what he had to do or how he was going to stop the planes.

CHAPTER NINE

Benedicto pushed the boat into the water as the men jumped in and waited for him to follow. The Guardian Angel waved his hands around as he created some wind to propel the boat forward quicker.

The men hung on to the sides as the boat swiftly passed through the water with barely a ripple. They exchanged worried glances back and forth but didn't say a word for fear of falling out of the boat or angering the huge man who commanded the wind to obey him.

When they arrived back on Candle Island everyone was sitting on the sand with Branyrd facing them and gesturing with her hands. She stopped in mid-sentence when she saw Benedicto and the men alighting out of the boat and hurrying forward.

She waited to hear what had happened and how receptive the ruler of the big island was to their requests for peace.

Benedicto motioned to Branyrd to come closer so he could explain what had transpired.

"You are making me nervous, Benedicto. Please tell me what happened."

"Soon enough, Angel. But first we must make sure that all the people here on the island are safe inside in case..."

"In case what?" she asked in alarm.

"Well, the ruler was somewhat receptive to our demands to stop the war but the problem is he is not the one sending the planes with bombs."

"What? Who is responsible for this destruction and death?"

"That I do not know yet. Kamalnayo, the ruler, said that he is not the one sending the planes and that they do not even have any planes or bombs. These planes are coming from another island that wants to take over the Peeples Islands. Kamalnayo agreed only if they took Candle Island and left the rest of the Peeples island alone. But it doesn't look like they did this for the planes bombed one of his islands too."

"Oh no! Now what? What island is doing this? We must find out and stop them."

"Yes, we will find them and do that soon, Angel. In the meantime, make sure everyone is comfortable inside. We will have to build some more huts since these are overcrowded as it is."

"Are you good at building huts, Benedicto?"

"I will figure out a way to do that."

"Wait a minute. How did you convince the ruler to stop the war? I know there is more to this story."

"Yes, HE helped me convince Kamalnayo of what he must do to bring peace to the islands. The ruler has a son who was gravely ill. HE healed him. This gift to the ruler helped to convince the ruler that he must do all he can to stop the devastation on the islands."

"But what can Kamalnayo do to convince this other island to stop this war? If they take over this island, what will happen to these natives? Will they be killed too? We must do something to help them take care of themselves."

"Yes, I agree, Angel. You will teach them how to protect themselves. We will build them some homes to stay in and give them what they will need to survive."

"We do not have weapons or anything like that, Benedicto. Remember, we are peaceful Angels."

"Of course, Branyrd. I know that but we will have to come up with a way to deter any more aggression toward them until the ruler can come to an agreement with the island in question."

"Why didn't he tell you more about the island, dammit…I mean darn it? If we knew the name of the island and where it is located, we could go there and reason with the leaders."

Benedicto gave her his sternest face in reprimand and then said, "Well, we will go this route first. This is what HE wants us to do for now. HE will lead us in the right direction, don't you worry."

"I'm sorry for that slip but I always worry, Benedicto. You know me." Branyrd smirked at him and he in turn gave her a quirky eyebrow lift. She still couldn't fathom how he performed this weird maneuver.

The islanders were busy discussing what happened on the main island after they were told all about it by the visiting natives who witnessed the miracle.

They looked at the huge man, gawked and whispered, wanting to know more about how he did that and if he would do more.

One man stepped forward and asked Benedicto, "How did you raise the ruler's son from his sick bed on the island? This boy has been dying for many months, getting weaker and sicker with each passing day. They did everything they could to heal him even their shaman could not bring him back to good health."

Branyrd turned to the man and answered for her Guardian Angel after Benedicto pointed to her, "Our LORD is all powerful and all knowing. HE can do anything. All good things come from HIM to those who believe and pray to HIM in HIS name."

"If we all pray to your god, will HE listen to us especially now in our time of need?"

"HE always listens to all who pray. HE will help you in ways you don't realize. HE is helping you now by sending us to assist you, answer your questions and pray with you."

"What about those men and women who died? How come HE did not help them?"

"HE decides who is to live or die. If someone's time is over here on Earth HE will come down and take them to live with

HIM in Heaven. They will not feel pain or suffering anymore. They will live in peace and happiness always."

The natives were quiet as they contemplated what the giant man had told them. They kept their eyes on him wherever he moved so as not to miss another miracle.

Benedicto could feel their eyes on him and knew what was in their hearts – fear and yet doubt of what had transpired, at least in those who were not witnesses to the miracle. He and Branyrd had much to do to convince them to believe in something greater than them.

Branyrd opened her mind to Benedicto when he glanced her way. "Do not worry about them. They still doubt that we can help them. But we will get it done and keep them all safe from harm."

"I hope so, Benedicto. I find that I am doubting myself and my ability to complete this mission. Where do we go from here?"

Benedicto gave her his best smile and shrugged his shoulders.

"Oh, you can get me so exasperated at times, Benedicto!" Branyrd sighed heavily and sat down on the sand next to the children. Maybe if I talk to them, I will feel better."

CHAPTER TEN

Dack looked up at the Angel and smiled. He patted her hand and said, "Don't look sad, Branyrd, I am here to help you."

Branyrd giggled at this young child's words of comfort. "That is very kind of you to say, Dack. I appreciate that. We all need support. Will you be my support?"

"Yep! I am a good supporter." Dack's brilliant smile softened the sadness that the Angel was feeling at that moment.

"Can I ask you a question, Dack?"

"Sure. I hope I can answer you," the boy said with a quizzical expression of curiosity on his face.

"Well, I remember you knew one of the soldiers that brought us here. You said he was your uncle. I thought you were an orphan."

"Yes, I am an orphan after my uncle died. He used to take care of me after my parents died."

"But if he is dead…then…" Branyrd gasped and covered her mouth but her eyes showed her surprise.

"What is wrong, Branyrd?" Dack asked in surprise.

"Oh nothing. Everything is fine."

Branyrd called out to Benedicto's mind to inform him of this revelation. "Would you believe that? The soldiers didn't exist. No wonder the old couple were surprised when we mentioned that the soldiers took us there. There were no soldiers. It was HIM!"

"Yes, Angel. It was. Do you not believe that HE is with us even now? I did tell you that they were sent by HIM."

"Yes, you did. I guess I must think of the impossible even if…well, I am acting human again, Benedicto. Sorry about that. I am supposed to be an Angel 1st Class. What is wrong with me? Nothing HE does should surprise me!"

"There you go! Now you are thinking correctly once again. Good job, Angel."

"What do we do now, Benedicto? I wish I had more confidence in myself. I did better in my last mission. I thought that was a difficult one, but it was a piece of cake compared to this."

"No, it won't be once you get your mind around what is happening to these people, you will know what to do next."

"I hope so. But you are always here for me too, right?"

"Of course, Angel. I am always just a thought or whisper away. Just whisper my name and I will be here."

"But…where are you going? Aren't you going to stay here with me?" Branyrd asked in alarm.

"I think it is time for me to leave you alone to figure out the rest. I did my part but will be here when you need me again. Don't worry. HE has confidence in you. That is what is important here."

Branyrd glanced around and noticed that her Guardian Angel had disappeared as he always did in each of her missions. *I think he is trying to tell me something, that I can do this on my own. But, can I?*

Seth, Freya and Dack came running over to the Angel. Seth looked up at her and asked, "Where did the giant man go? He was just here a minute ago? Can he do magic? Can you?"

"Oh, you mean Benedicto? He is around here somewhere. I think he had to do something to help us find our way out of here. He will be back again, don't worry." But the Angel was worried.

A drone of incoming planes could be heard overhead as one dipped close to where Branyrd was standing on the beach along with the children. She hurriedly told them, "Go back to the huts and wait until I come get you."

She gazed up as the plane settled down to land in a nearby field. Two people came out and headed her way. She looked around to find Benedicto once again but to no avail. She would have to handle this by herself. She pulled her shoulders back and took a deep cleansing breath and said a mantra of, "I can do this; I can do this! Oh LORD, please help me do this!"

The two men stopped a few feet in front of the Angel and spoke, "Sorry to frighten you, miss. We are here to speak with you about what transpired on the other island. The ruler sent us here to make peace with you. Are you the one who brought the son of Kamalnayo back to life?"

"No, I am not. HE is the one who did that. Are you natives from the Peeples Island?"

"HE, who is HE? We are from another island. Kamalnayo made a deal with us that we could take over his islands too and join them to ours in solidarity. Many islands working together are stronger than a few alone."

"HE is the one and only one who can do such things. What you are saying is not what I heard. I think that you have something else in mind. You want to control these islands and decimate the inhabitants and transform these islands into something to benefit you and you alone."

The men appeared confused at her words but responded, "No, you are wrong. We are not here to harm anyone."

"How do you explain all the deaths and damage to the island here?" Branyrd was feeling stronger as her voice grew in pitch and her face glowed.

The two men backed away and bowed their heads afraid to look at her since the light emanating behind her hurt their eyes.

"We did not want to do any of this. Our leader told us that we had to do this. We had no choice. Our island is sinking and we need another archipelago to move to."

"Why weren't you honest with Kamalnayo? He would have helped you and allowed your people to come here."

"There is not enough room for all of us on this island. That is why we had to rid the island of its natives, to make room. We promise to rebuild and let the rest of them stay. We will work something out."

Branyrd silently asked for help from above. "What do I do now, LORD? How will this work? Will there be enough room for all of them here? Will they be able to live in peace once the natives here find out these men were responsible for the deaths of their loved ones?"

Benedicto was listening at a distance behind the men and came forward. Once the men spotted the giant, they backed away more and looked up at the Guardian Angel in awe.

"Who are you?" the men asked in surprise.

"I am Benedicto and here to protect these people along with Branyrd."

"Who is Branyrd?" one man queried.

"She stands before you."

Branyrd smiled and sighed in relief. "I am Branyrd. We are both here to protect all these natives and take back their home."

"Do you think that you two can stop us from taking all this over?" one man bravely asked.

"Yes, without a doubt because HE is on our side."

"Again, you mention HE. Who is HE?"

"HE is here now. Why don't you ask HIM," Branyrd said with a smirk as she felt HIS presence all around them.

The men looked back and forth and shook their heads. "There is no one else here but us. What are you trying to do, confuse us?"

A spark came out of the sky and hit the plane in the field causing it to explode into flames.

The men jumped back in alarm and cried out, "What did you do? How did you do that? How are we going to get back to our island?"

"HE did that! You don't need to go back. This is your island now too, at least that is what you said." Branyrd stifled a snicker.

"We...we...need to get back right away. They are waiting for your reply."

"This is our reply. You will not take over this island. If you want to come here in peace to live with the other natives, then that is the only way you will be welcome here. You must also help them bury their dead, apologize to them for what you did to their homes and rebuild them all."

"But...but...we cannot do that. We are only two men. How can we do that? Our leader will kill us now if we don't go back there."

"Where is there?" Benedicto asked as he leaned closer to the men meeting their eyes.

"We live a distance from here beyond the last of the Peeples Islands. It is called Wanalami. The volcano erupted and is smothering the island on one side. All the people have moved to the other side and now the Earth has erupted there also. We have nowhere else to go. You must help us. Can HE do something to stop the volcano?"

"HE can do anything as long as you pray and believe in HIM."

"But we don't even know who HE is or where HE is. We can't see HIM. How do we believe in something we cannot see?"

"But you did see your plane explode, did you not?" Branyrd asked.

"Yes…yes…we did, but we did not see HIM do it."

"You do not need to see HIM to believe in HIM," Branyrd responded with a steely-eyed gaze.

The men could not look at her and bowed their heads as they began to plead on their hands and knees.

CHAPTER ELEVEN

In the distance Branyrd spotted a large boat heading their way. There was a man standing at the helm wearing a hat with colorful feathers and holding a long sword.

Benedicto stood at the water's edge waiting for the boat to come closer. As it did, he recognized Kamalnayo. He was anything but happy when he spotted the two men standing with Branyrd. By the expression on Kamalnayo's face, the ruler knew who these men were, trouble, nothing but trouble.

"What brings you here, Kamalnayo?" Benedicto queried.

"I saw the plane coming over and I knew who it was. These two men came to my island at the request of their leader to convince me to betray my own people. I've made a terrible mistake even if I was at odds with my people over some insignificant things like medicine, taxes and such. I have come to make amends with my people. I had no idea this other island would harm my people."

The natives came out of the huts when they saw Kamalnayo walking onto the beach. They were too curious to stay inside for long.

The ruler stood close to the two startled men who stepped back in alarm. They noticed the displeasure on the ruler's face and were not sure what he would do to them now that they were stranded there.

"Why are you here? Kamalnayo asked.

One man stuttered and cleared his throat before continuing, "We are sorry for the trouble we caused you and your people. We did not want to harm anyone. We only wanted to find a place to bring our people who are in grave danger of dying on our island."

"Do you know what you did to my people?" Kamalnayo raised his voice in anger as he quizzed them and looked around at the natives gathering beside him and the devastation in the distance. "You have killed many people and destroyed their homes leaving them here now without anything to survive. What do you say for yourselves?"

The second man answered without looking the ruler in the eye, "We have apologized for what we have done and will continue to do so to all who are here. We did not want to do this. Our leader forced us or else he said he would let our families die on our island. Time is of the essence; we need to get off our sinking island. People are in boats waiting to come here. They have nowhere else to go. We were sent here to make sure that it is safe for our people now that it has been cleared."

"Do you plan to harm any more of my people when you all arrive?"

"No, of course not. We promise with our lives to keep them all safe. If we don't go back to our island soon our leader will think that he needs to send more bombs here."

"I will go there with you by boat and meet with him. If I can't convince him to stop this war, then I will kill him myself. There is no reason why we cannot all live in peace after he makes restitution for what he did. I don't know if my people will ever forgive him for what has happened though. Many have lost their families and homes that can never be replaced."

A grumbling of agreement was heard from all the natives gathered there.

"I understand. I would feel the same if I lost my family and home. What can we do to help you?" the first man asked.

"You will come with me to speak to your leader."

The two men assented and followed Kamalnayo to the boat where Branyrd stood waiting next to Benedicto.

"I will go with you, Kamalnayo," Benedicto stated as he leaped into the boat.

"Do you want me to come too, Benedicto?" Branyrd asked, not sure why he was doing this.

"Stay with the natives and keep them safe. I will return as soon as possible."

Once all were in the boat, Benedicto blew the sails and propelled the boat forward much to the chagrin of the men handling the sails who were tossed about but thankfully not off the boat.

The men looked on in awe as the boat moved so swiftly that they had to hold on for dear life.

Branyrd watched from the shore and giggled, for she knew how fast Benedicto could move an object. She had felt what it was like to fly and not be able to stop until he was ready.

The natives on shore spoke excitedly and pointed to the flying boat in their own languages as they wore smiles of amusement and the children laughed out loud.

"Can we go for a ride next, Branyrd?" Seth asked in wonder.

"Well, maybe if we ask Benedicto when he comes back," she responded with a chuckle.

"How does he do that, Branyrd?" Dack questioned as he kept watching the boat disappear.

"HE does that for Benedicto. Only HE can do such things."

"Where is HE? Why doesn't HE come here so we can see HIM?

"HE is here."

"What? Where? I don't see HIM?" Dack whirled around in surprise.

Branyrd laughed at the innocence of youth. "HE is right here each time you think of HIM, pray to HIM or call HIS name for help," the Angel said pointing to Dack's chest.

Dack looked at his chest and puffed it out. "I still don't see HIM or feel HIM here." He rubbed his chest to make sure.

"As long as you believe in HIM, Dack, and say your prayers every night HE will always be right here." Branyrd touched Dack's chest again where his heart was.

"Oh, you mean HE will be inside my heart? There isn't room there for HIM, is there?"

"There is always room for one more in your heart, especially HIM."

Dack shrugged his shoulders and looked at the other children who came forward to look at the boy's chest and feel it to make sure there was no one there.

***

While Branyrd waited for Benedicto's return, she worked with the natives and the children to put together some more huts. Mortan and Miriam who appeared to be the leaders here pointed to some of the palm trees and instructed the Angels and the others to use the downed trees and cut down more of the palm trees to use them to build. Mortan was a craftsman and a master carver. He could make anything out of a piece of wood and learned this skill from his father and grandfather.

Branyrd prayed the whole time she was working for help in getting these huts built as strong and sturdy as possible in a short time. She was so wrapped up in building, that she didn't notice the others standing back and now watching her put together huts so fast that her hands were flying. When she heard sounds of ooh and aah she stopped working to look around.

The natives clapped their hands and bowed to her in praise for the excellent work she had performed. There stood a dozen huts in all sizes, some larger than the others but all sturdy and well-built.

She snickered and smiled at them. "I didn't do all this on my own. You helped me and so did HE." She pointed upward to the sky. The natives followed her finger to see what she was pointing at.

They nodded and smiled back at her but still looked a little skeptical for they knew she had done most of it herself.

Branyrd instructed the men to move the huts to a location where they would be protected by the other trees around them. Children hurried inside each hut to check them over. They laid more palm leaves on the floors of each hut to finish them off as instructed by the old couple who rewarded them with some sliced fruit and coconut milk.

It was getting late and the sun would be going down with no sign of Benedicto. The natives built a fire and began preparing their dinner with a whole pig that they had saved up for this occasion. Many of the other animals had been destroyed in the fires but many other animals may have escaped and wandered the island now. There was much to celebrate, for peace would hopefully return when the large man came back.

Branyrd sat down on the sand near the water and prayed that her Guardian Angel would be back soon with good news. She believed that HE would not forsake them but prayed continually as she scanned the horizon for any sign.

For some reason HE was not letting her know anything now and was keeping her in suspense. She turned to look at the natives when she smelled the aromas of the pork cooking over a spit. She had never smelled anything so good in her life, or at least her human life while she was here on Earth. She never felt hungry, but for some reason she did now. She would try some of this meat when it was ready to be served. After all, the natives would be insulted if she didn't at least try some.

A ruckus was heard suddenly from the people who pointed out to sea; she returned her attention to the horizon where several long boats were spotted coming their way.

CHAPTER TWELVE

The Sisters of Love gathered all the children together to keep them safe in case there was trouble from the boats. Seth, Freya and Dack held hands and stood close to Branyrd with Seth's and Freya's parents behind them. Misty, barked a warning as his hair stood on end.

Seth was whispering to his father, "What is going to happen, Daddy? Are they coming to kill us?"

"Oh no, Seth. We will be fine. Benedicto is at the helm. See him? He is moving his hands to propel the boats forward faster."

"I like how he does that, Daddy! I hope he will take me, Freya and Dack for a ride soon."

"I'm sure he will if you ask him. But please don't bother him just yet. He will want to tell us about what the leader of the other island said first."

"Ok, Daddy. But I hope he can talk fast because I don't think I can wait long," Seth sighed in anticipation.

His father patted his son on the head but kept his eyes peeled on the large man as he came forward. "Keep Misty close to you and don't let him near the men."

"All right, Daddy. Will they hurt Misty?"

"Not if you hold him here."

Seth nodded as Freya came alongside him to help.

Benedicto stepped out of the boat almost effortlessly like on a cloud and took Branyrd aside. He whispered, "There is a lot to tell you, Angel. We need to keep the natives from both islands calm until we can work something out."

"Of course. I can do that." Branyrd said with a questioning look.

"There is plenty to tell you, be patient, Angel." Benedicto stepped forward and exclaimed, "Wow! Have you built all those huts since I left?"

"Yes. We did. Do you like them?"

"They are magnificent, Angel! You outdid yourself. Did you do that alone or with some help?" Benedicto raised his eyebrow in his inimitable way.

"Well, I couldn't do it alone. We all did it with HIS help, of course."

"Nice, very nice indeed!" The Guardian Angel stepped in and out of each hut and smiled with pleasure. These will do just fine. We have plenty of people in the boats that will need a hut for their families. We will have to build more though, I think."

'No problem, Benedicto. I'll get right on it. How large do you think they should be and how many do we need?"

The Guardian Angel counted the people getting off the many boats that were coming ashore. Some of them gathered in families and he surmised that they would need at least another two dozen more huts.

"Are all the people safely off the island now, Benedicto?"

"No, there are more coming behind us. We may have to take some of the boats back to get the rest of them though. We couldn't put too many in each boat or we would sink. I put in many more than I should have and have had HIS help keeping them afloat."

"Yes, I can see that," the Angel said as she watched more people coming off the last boat that was also overloaded with supplies.

"Let me get these people settled in the huts, then I can see how many more we will need." Branyrd greeted the natives and directed them to pick out huts to suit their needs. "If you need a larger hut with more rooms, please let me know. I will be building more shortly."

The men looked in awe at this small woman who said she would build more huts. They couldn't believe she had built these. They were better than their own huts on the island they just left and they told her so in their own language.

Branyrd listened to them and responded back in their language with the help of the LORD, much to their surprise.

"How do you know our language, beautiful lady?" one woman asked.

Branyrd tried to explain, "Our LORD is showing me how to do that and leading the way for us to get along. It is easier to do that if we can converse and understand one another in each other's languages. I can speak whatever language HE allows me to speak to make this possible."

"Who is our LORD?" one man asked in confusion.

Again, Branyrd used his language and answered, "HE is the Almighty and has put all of us here on this Earth for a purpose. HE is the one that we pray to when we need help like now."

"Do you mean that if I pray for help this person would listen to me and grant my wishes?"

"Well, that all depends on what you wish for. If HE thinks that those wishes are necessary then HE may grant them. But it is all up to HIM. We have no say in anything. We are just here because HE put us here. That is why Benedicto and I, Branyrd, are here to help you, at HIS request."

"The large man told us something like that too when we asked him who he was and where he came from. He is the largest man we have ever seen. We are not large people as you can see. We are all small. Our largest person is the man over there helping lift the cooked pig off the spit. He is also the strongest man we have."

Branyrd looked at the man who was lifting the cooked pig like it didn't weigh much. He placed it on the table where the women began cutting it and putting pieces on palm leaves as plates to pass around to everyone.

She nodded and smiled. "I will need your help too to get huts ready for the rest of your people. Can you clear some of the land over there and get it ready for huts?"

Several men stepped forward along with some of the women, who looked as if they could handle any task, to help Branyrd and went right to work.

"We are indebted to you, Branyrd," one woman said as she bowed in front of the Angel and took her hand in hers to hold tightly. "You must be an Angel to do all this for us after what we have done to this island. We will clean it up and do all we can to help the people here. We had no right to harm them or take their homes. We were frightened about dying and listened to our leader when he said he would find us a new home. We did not know that he would destroy the homes of these poor people. How can we make amends?"

"That is up to the people here on Candle Island and those on the neighboring island chain of the Peeples Islands. The leader, Kamalnayo is here. Maybe you should speak to him about this. He is over there with the children."

"Okay, we will do that now. Thank you, Branyrd, for all you are doing to make us feel welcome here on our new home." The woman bowed to the Angel and backed away as she headed over to see Kamalnayo along with several of her fellow natives.

Branyrd directed her attention back to making more huts as fast as she could with the help of Mortan and the other islanders who kept bringing her more supplies of palm trees and leaves. The men watched her as she finished one small hut and began the next. They copied what she was doing with a little help from Branyrd. She asked HIM to move their hands quickly like hers.

One man looked up in alarm as his hands began to move quicker than he thought possible. He tried to stop them but became frightened when he could not.

Branyrd came over to him and placed her hands on his and stopped them from moving. She explained, "HE is helping you complete the task as fast as possible so that we can get all the people safely into huts before too late. There are more of your people coming now. Look!"

"Thank you, Branyrd. I did not know what was happening to me. Yes, I see them more coming now. The other men are also having the same difficulty stopping their hands."

"Don't worry, I will help them. We have completed several huts already and have several more to finish. You can go at a slower pace now. Okay?"

"Yes, I think I like the slower pace myself. I will finish up some of the beds inside instead while you do the huts themselves. Okay?"

Mortan heard the man speak of making the beds and announced, "I will help you. I am a master carver and working together we will complete these tasks quickly."

"That's perfect. Good idea. Thank you, Mortan. All the huts will need furniture. The rest of the men will help you do that to finish up as quickly as possible."

"I plan to get them all to help. We are proficient at making furniture out of palm trees and leaves," one man stated proudly.

A few hours later all was finished and each family had their own hut with furniture included inside. The pig was almost gone along with plenty of vegetables and fruits that the women had passed around for dessert. The children were yawning and slowly falling asleep in their parent's or the nuns' arms as they were carried inside the huts for the night. Even Misty had his fill of pork and was snoozing in the sand until Seth and Freya woke him to bring him into their hut for the night.

The ruler, Kamalnayo, was in deep discussion with the ruler of the disappearing island, Wanalami, now as their voices raised in disagreements.

Branyrd glanced around for Benedicto and found him with several natives who were still in awe of his size and power. He was helping them lift the boats out of the water and put them on the shore so that they would not float away. Once all the boats were safely moored, he turned to see Branyrd watching him.

"Hello, Angel. I was going to find you once I finished this task. Did you try some of that pork?"

Branyrd shook her head, "Not yet. I was so busy with the huts that I forgot all about it. But I promise to try some before it is all gone. It did smell delicious when it was roasting on the spit."

"I tried it and liked it. It's not something I will ever have again since I don't see us coming back here."

"It's sad to say that, isn't it, Benedicto?"

"Yes, it is sad to leave a place, but I like to think back on all we have learned from these people. We are not yet done here with your mission, Angel, remember that. There is still much work to do."

"Are you going to share what happened on the other island?"

"Yes, it is time to tell you," Benedicto sighed. "There is much to share, Angel. Some you may like but other things you may not."

"What does that mean, Guadian Angel?"

"Peace is not assured yet. The leaders are still arguing about who will be in control. At least the planes are gone and will not return with bombs, instead they will be bringing supplies from other islands here to help rebuild some of the buildings that were destroyed. The planes were from some other islands that Marnolani borrowed for the purpose of taking over this island."

"That is too bad that he had to do that but good to hear that he is trying to make amends, Benedicto. I wondered about that. It will take a long time to get things back to normal, if ever."

"Yes, that is true. But maybe things had to change eventually. Now all the people will have to learn to get along here on this island and the rest of the archipelago."

The island was quiet as all were settled in their huts but there was something brewing in the distance.

CHAPTER THIRTEEN

Branyrd and Benedicto checked in with each hut to make sure everyone was comfortable and not in need of anything. This was the time to think about what their next task would be.

"I think we should be trying to help those in the village of this island rebuild. I feel as if I could do some more building there with HIS help."

"Yes, I think you could, Branyrd. You have become quite adept at building huts. Do you think you could build larger buildings now?" Benedicto smirked at her.

"Well, I don't know. But with HIS help, I can do anything," Branyrd gushed but bent her head in shame. "I know I am not supposed to feel pride but after seeing all the work on the huts here I feel a little. Sorry about that, LORD. I will try harder not to feel that emotion."

"It only makes you more human and vulnerable, Angel."

"I guess so. But I can't seem to stop these human feelings from surfacing. What can I do?"

"You must ask HIM. Only HE can forgive your sins. Let HIM tell you what HE expects of you."

"I plan to do that since I feel helpless unless I am doing something productive while I am here."

Branyrd sat down on the water's edge letting her feet touch the water as it came closer to her. It felt so peaceful and serene looking out over the ocean that she almost fell asleep. This was not something she needed to do as an Angel, but her human emotions were filling her up and making her relax.

"Angel, listen to ME!"

"Oh, LORD, I am listening. Sorry, I felt as if I was going to fall asleep. It is so peaceful and calming here with the water lapping at my feet and the sand still warm from the sun under my body."

"So, I see, Angel. You are not finished with this mission. I appreciate what you have done so far preaching to these people about ME. I have been hearing many prayers because of that. Good job, Angel. I have been busy listening and granting their wishes as needed. But one has ME wondering."

"Wondering? I didn't think YOU ever had to wonder, LORD. YOU know everything."

"Yes, I do, Angel, but this is something that I want you to handle."

"What do you want me to do, LORD?" Branyrd felt a nervous tingle inside her that she had never felt before. It made her shake all over with…was it fear?

"Yes, Angel. It is fear. I think you have felt another human emotion. It is not a pleasant one this time though. I will help dispel it from you. Relax and take a deep breath, Branyrd, and it will go away."

"Okay, yes, I feel better now. Thank you, LORD. Why did I feel this emotion of fear. It is not a good feeling. Now I know what all the people here have been feeling. It is not something I ever want to feel again."

"That is why I made you feel it so you would know what it feels like. Knowing this feeling will help you understand what the people here have been going through losing their families and homes and not knowing what will happen to them next."

"I understand now, LORD. I have felt happiness, sadness, peacefulness and now fearfulness. It is the worst feeling of all. What can I do to help these people dispel this feeling?"

"Well, you must go back to the destroyed village and check on the building to see if you can help them along as you did with the huts. I will guide your hands to move and build what is needed. There is a storm coming this way and the people must be in stronger huts away from the beach for the water will come in and take them all away."

"Oh no, that can't happen, LORD! Can't you stop it?"

"Yes, I could but I want the people here to find a way to work together in peace for a common good. If a storm comes, this will force them to do that with your help. Take Benedicto with you so you can both work throughout the night to rebuild some of the village to make it safe for the people to return."

"Right away, LORD. I did mention something like this to Benedicto."

"Yes, I heard that. Who do you think put those thoughts in your head?"

"Oh, of course. I didn't come up with that on my own. Thank you, LORD."

"You did get the idea brewing inside that head of yours before I saw it and cultivated it. I will give you some credit, Angel." A tittering could be heard as HIS voice disappeared.

"Benedicto, come here quickly." Branyrd looked around for her Guardian Angel but he was nowhere in sight.

"For goodness sakes, Benedicto! Where are you?"

"You called, Angel?" Benedicto appeared behind Branyrd and tapped her on the shoulder.

"Oh, you frightened me half to death, Benedicto! Why do you do that? Damn...I mean for Pete's sake!"

"Good catch, Angel. That was a close one. You are doing so much better than before. I know HE has noticed this too."

"I'm sure HE has. Now where did you go? I just had a discussion with HIM about what we must do next. Do you want to hear it or do you know already?" Branyrd raised her brows and wiggled them at him.

"Please share this with me, Branyrd. I am all ears."

She swore that Benedicto's ears suddenly got bigger.

"What did you just do?"

"Oh nothing. I am listening. Are you going to tell me what we must do next?"

"Hmm, okay, if you will get serious again and listen."

"Like I said, I am all ears!" Benedicto gave her his quirky brow, wiggled his ears, and smiled.

Branyrd sighed and explained what the LORD had told her must be done and soon before the impending storm hit the island. The two Angels headed to the part of the devastated island to make reparations and begin the building. There were many men there pulling supplies out of the planes and beginning to rebuild one of the buildings. The planes lifted off and returned to their islands before the storm.

The two Angels joined in. The night flew by but the Angels kept working. The noise was heard by the natives on the beach in the wee hours who followed the sounds and came upon the two Angels working with their hands flying in all directions as they built houses where there once stood a devastated village.

The men called out to others as they came by the dozens to help the Angels rebuild their homes and create a new village. The children followed closely behind to do what they were told to do, find more palm leaves and whatever else they could find to fill in the holes in the floors of the buildings. They worked together throughout the morning and only stopped to have some refreshments provided by the women who were now also there to help.

Misty barked at everyone and greeted the women warmly when they offered him something to eat. He received plenty of pats on the head and scratches behind the ears as he licked their hands of any food left behind.

Seth, Freya and Dack and the rest of the children gathered what wood they could find in the rubble and dropped these off to the men and Angels as they rushed back and forth as more was requested.

Everyone had a job to do and all were getting along. Even the leaders, who had quarreled the day before and still not settled with what they were going to do, were now barking out orders to everyone to keep working. They were even seen lifting large piles of supplies and moving them closer to the workers.

The wind was picking up and blowing around any loose materials. The children became frightened and rushed to Branyrd's and Benedicto's side for protection.

"Listen everyone," Branyrd announced, "we need to hurry and get all the children inside the houses now. Some of you come with me. We must bring all the huts away from the beach and closer to the larger buildings so that they will not get washed away."

The largest native stepped forward and said, "I will bring them, Branyrd, with Benedicto's help. I know I can't do it alone."

More natives gathered around and offered to help their fellow islander do what was necessary. The other natives new to the island lined up behind and followed them to help. Even the two men who came over in the plane were doing their share.

Branyrd smiled and looked up and said, "It's working, LORD. I think it's working. Please keep the storm back until we can get everyone safely inside."

The Angel's words were swept away by the high winds that began buffeting them and making it difficult to stand. The children held onto to Branyrd as she pulled them into the larger new huts and closed the doors. The sisters waved her away and said, "We will stay here to make sure they are safe. Don't worry!"

"Thank you, Sisters. I will see if I can help the men on the beach get back here."

Branyrd felt her feet lift off the ground as she was thrown up into the air. She pulled herself this way and that and finally landed back down on the sand. Those around her looked on in surprise when they saw her flying around.

CHAPTER FOURTEEN

"Can you fly, Angel?" one man asked as he hurried over to help her.

"No, I cannot fly here, only in Heaven. It was the wind. It is so strong that I could not keep my feet on the ground."

"Oh, I see. But where is Heaven?" the man asked, confused.

"That is the place that we all go to when we leave this world."

"Is it a good place to go?"

"Yes, the very best place of all."

"Will I go there?"

"Yes, I believe you will. You are a good man, are you not?"

"Yes, yes, I am!" the man answered quickly.

"Well, then you will go there, the LORD willing."

The man nodded, smiled, and left her side after making sure that she was not going to fly away again.

Benedicto came over to check on her. "Are you all right, Angel?"

"Yes, I couldn't stand up. The wind took me away. It was a little exhilarating but at the same time frightening. I know what fear feels like now."

"Do you?" Benedicto asked with a smirk.

"Yes, he allowed me to feel that so I could sympathize and empathize with the people here."

"I see," he smiled at her. "Well, Angel, try to keep your feet on the ground. Okay? Will you be all right now?" he chuckled as he walked back to continue pulling the huts away from the beach.

"Sometimes I wonder about you, Benedicto. Were you sent along with me to torment and tease me?"

Benedicto's chuckle could be heard in the wind as Branyrd headed over to assist in any way she could to bring the huts closer to the other buildings.

The men and women pulled and pushed the huts over logs of palm trees as the sweat dried off their backs in the wind. It was getting more difficult to stand up and they found by holding onto one another and forming a chain they could move better.

Once they had moved the last hut closer to the other buildings, they all went inside and gathered their families close as the winds continued to batter the buildings that swayed and vibrated but held strong.

Things were not as safe out on the water where a lone boat was knocked around and nearly tipped over in the increasing waves. Two adults and two children held onto one another as they prayed that they would reach the shore before they were capsized.

Branyrd listened to the wind and heard the rain pelting the roof of the hut she and Benedicto were in. She moved outside and pulled him with her.

"There is someone out there in the water. We must help them, Benedicto."

"Yes, I can hear their cries. Come with me, Angel."

Before she could agree her Guardian Angel whisked her up in the air and flew them to the water where they hovered above the boat that was slowing sinking.

The children were being held up above the water by their parents as they cried out for help.

When one of the children looked up and spotted the two people hovering over the boat, he reached out his hands to them. "Look, there is someone up there. I think they want to help us, Daddy!"

"What? How is that possible?" the man asked in confusion.

"Look, Mareka, there are two people flying above us. How can that be? Am I dreaming? Do you see them?"

"Yes, how can they be up there? What is holding them up?"

"Reach your hands out to us," Branyrd said in a loud voice so they could hear her over the wind.

"Are you real?" the little girl asked as she reached out her hand.

"Yes, we are real. Reach out your hands now and we will help you," Benedicto said as he reached out with his large hands and pulled the children up out of the sinking boat.

Branyrd reached down and pulled first the mother and then the father keeping them close together as they flew back to the shore.

"How could you do this?" the father asked as they lay on the sand. He hugged his wife and children to him as they cried in relief.

"No time to explain now. Please come with us to safety. You cannot stay here on the beach. The storm is getting stronger and the winds will take you away," Branyrd announced as she gripped the children's hands and pulled them along as Benedicto grabbed the parents and did the same.

Once back to the huts and other buildings, the family was directed to a safe place and tucked away there with others to comfort them.

Voices were raised in shock as the family recounted their near-death-experiences in the small boat and the miraculous rescue by these two people who must surely be Angels.

The other natives just smiled and nodded. "Yes, they truly are Angels."

The man responded, "What? But how?"

"We do not ask how but are thankful," one woman stated with a sigh.

CHAPTER FIFTEEN

There was a cry of alarm from Seth and Freya as they looked around the hut for their dog Misty.

"Where is he? I can't find Misty, Daddy! Where did he go? He was just here a minute ago," Seth cried out, tears flooding his eyes.

Freya looked around and asked everyone, "Have you seen our dog, Misty? He was here and now he is gone."

Their parents looked underneath the beds, table and chairs and behind others who were sitting on the floor. The hut was crowded but no one had seen the dog.

"Oh no, Mommy! What are we going to do? Where could he have gone?"

The parents exchanged worried glances and whispered, "We have to go out there to find him."

"No, you stay here, I will go," the father said to his wife and turning to his children, "I will find Misty. Don't worry. Stay here with your mother. I will be back as soon as I can with him."

Seth and Freya looked up and said, "Please LORD, if you can hear us, please save our dog. His name is Misty. We love him so much and don't want him to die. Please save him and keep our father safe too."

Branyrd was listening to the prayers when the LORD opened a channel for her. She smiled and said, "I will find Misty, LORD, with your help. Do you know where he is?"

"Yes, but wait. I will be close behind the father to keep him safe until he finds the dog."

All this time Misty was hiding inside a broken-down hut not far from where his family was. He had gone outside when the new family came in because he had to relieve himself. What happened was he could not go back inside once the door was closed. He huddled close to the ground and crawled away until he found a hut that was in pieces but still enough to keep him from flying away. He shivered on the ground as he was pelted by the hard driving rain and high winds. He hugged the ground and lay there not knowing what else to do.

Misty sniffed the air and then lay down again. He started to drift off to sleep but was awakened again by the loud sound that was coming toward him. His ears perked up when he saw something flying around.

A palm tree had fallen over close to where he was laying and palm leaves and coconuts were falling around him. He ducked his head and covered it with his paws as he shivered in fear.

Back at their hut Seth and Freya continued to pray for their dog through the tears that they kept wiping away. Their mother consoled them and said, "Don't worry. Your father will find Misty. He is a smart dog. He will find a place to hide until the storm passes."

"Do you think that this LORD will hear our prayers and help Daddy find him?" Seth asked as he hugged his mother and cried on her shoulder.

She held him tight and patted his back. "Yes, I think HE did. I think HE will help your father find Misty."

Freya hugged her mother too and sniffled as she stayed close to her brother's side and held his hand. She smiled at Seth and said, "Misty will come home. I believe he will."

"I hope so, Freya. What are we going to do without him? I love him so much."

"I do too, Seth. I do too!" Freya cried as she hung onto her little brother's hand.

The storm continued to grow in strength as trees were felled and coconuts hit the roofs of the huts and rolled down onto the ground. Palm leaves buffeted the sides of the buildings and stuck there with the high winds that continued to blow relentlessly.

Everyone in the buildings or huts shivered as they all began to pray that the buildings they were in, would not blow away or get knocked down. They exchanged worried and fearful expressions and held onto one another for comfort.

In another hut Branyrd and Benedicto whispered, "We need to go out there now. We must to help find Misty. The children are frantic with worry as well as their mother who is also concerned about her husband's safety."

"Angel, HE is there to take care of that. HE told us not to worry. We need to keep everyone inside until the worst of the storm has passed."

"Yes, I know, Benedicto. But I can't just sit here. We are Angels. We can do this. We don't need to stay inside. You can fly and so can I. Didn't you notice that I did recently?"

"Well, that was not you flying. That was the wind taking you for a ride, Angel." Benedicto snickered.

"Stop that right now, Guardian Angel. I have had enough of your teasing. I am going out there to help. You cannot stop me!"

"If you say so, Angel. Go right ahead." Benedicto moved away from the door for Branyrd to open it.

She tried and tried but could not open the door. The wind was so strong it kept it shut tight. She grunted and pulled and finally sighed. "Aren't you going to help me?"

"No. If HE wanted you to go out there, HE would have opened it for you, Angel."

"But why can't I go out there. I need to do something. I can't just sit here! Are you sure about that, Benedicto? Why doesn't HE want me to help?"

"I think HE has his reasons, Branyrd."

"Doesn't HE trust me to do HIS mission completely?"

"Oh, I think you already have, Angel. You have done all you can do for now. But I'm sure there will be more soon."

"What do you mean there will be more soon?"

"Wait and see, Angel. Wait and see."

CHAPTER SIXTEEN

On the island of Wanalami there were some stranded natives in the water. There were no more boats left and nowhere else for them to go. The last small boat left with a family of four before they and the rest of the stragglers could get to the boat. Now they were going to die in the water. They couldn't go back on land. The volcano was still spewing its molten lava all over the beach and it was now going into the water where steam was rising.

They had to keep swimming further out into the water to get away from the heat of the falling lava.

HE watched the men and women and a few children as they tried to stay afloat.

Branyrd opened her mind to HIM and begged, "Please, LORD, ask what YOU may of me. There must be something for me to do. Why can't I leave this building to help find the dog for the children. They are suffering."

"Yes, they are, Angel, but not for long. The dog will be returned to them by the father. I have made sure of that."

"But what can I do? I know that this mission has more for me to do. What do YOU want me to do now?"

"Be patient, Angel. I have more for you to do. Open the door and step out in the wind. Lift your feet up and fly to the island of Wanalami. It is there that you will find something that you must do."

***

Misty sniffed the air again and looked around. The wind was still buffeting the trees and sending palm leaves and coconuts in every direction. The rain was coming down harder than before but he could smell something familiar. He looked up and heard a voice. His tail wagged in delight as he realized who it was.

"There you are, Misty. I knew you would go somewhere safe. You are one smart dog. Come now. I will carry you back to the hut. The children miss you. Do you miss them too?"

The dog nodded as if he understood and snuggled against his master's chest as they struggled in the wind that threatened to knock them over and blow them away.

Back at the hut his family was praying and crying as they waited for their father and Misty to return safely.

Misty began to bark as the door opened and the father and dog went in to a joyous reunion. There was so much crying going on all around and then hugs, pats and scratches behind his ears to welcome Misty back.

"Thank you, Daddy! Thank you for bringing Misty back. I was worried that you would both be lost and blown away." Seth hugged his father and held onto Misty afraid to let him go.

"It's okay, Seth. I would miss Misty too if we lost him," his father responded with a smile.

"You can't go out again, Misty, until the wind stops blowing or you will be blown away. Okay?" Seth instructed as he gave his wet and happy dog another hug.

Freya rubbed Misty down with a cloth and hugged him as she told him, "I missed you, Misty, and love you so much! You will not go out until the storm is gone."

The dog smiled if a dog could smile and snuggled close to his beloved family. He had been relieved too to be home with them again but just couldn't tell them. He settled for licking their faces as they giggled.

Not far away there were others suffering and trying to survive.

CHAPTER SEVENTEEN

Branyrd did as she was requested by HIM. She opened the door this time without a problem and stepped out into the storm. She lifted her feet up and the wind took her up and away. She adjusted her body and went with the wind and settled into a swift ride on the currents.

She remembered how she had always wanted to learn how to fly on Earth and couldn't do it for a long time. But here she was flying like she was a pro without the help of Benedicto. She smiled and flew faster as she got closer to the glowing island that was almost completely under cover of the lava flow. Out in the water she spotted some heads bouncing up and down.

She headed down and hovered over the water as sparks were flying around and dropping into the water causing steam to rise and sizzle.

She called out to the people there, "Reach out your hands and I will help you."

"Look, there is a lady flying above us!" one man exclaimed as he held onto his son and daughter trying to keep them afloat with the help of his wife. Others were doing the same as they splashed around trying to keep away from the flying embers that kept dropping into the water around them.

"I am here to help you. You must reach out to me. I will pull you out."

"Where will you pull us? How can you do this?"

The father who was holding onto his son pushed his son's hands upward as he kept them both afloat. He didn't question the woman further, for what was happening did not make sense anyway. All he wanted was to keep his family safe and if this woman in the sky could do that he would not ask how.

Branyrd reached out and pulled the boy next to her. He held tightly to her neck afraid to fall back into the water. The man held up his daughter next and then went under. Branyrd managed to grip the girl's hand and pulled her up next to her brother. She flew closer to the water and reached in and pulled up the father and held onto his arm. She now had three people clinging to her neck and back as she reached down once again and pulled up the mother. She kept them all close to her. There were a few more bodies below struggling to stay afloat and crying out to her for help.

"I will get to you. I promise. Before she could turn and fly the family back to the shore of Candle Island, she nearly bumped into Benedicto. "Don't worry, Angel. I will get the rest of them. Head back and I will be right behind you."

"Oh, thank you, Benedicto. I didn't want to leave them but had no choice. I couldn't hold on to another person."

"That's why I am here. HE told me to come. There were too many in the water for you to take at once."

The family were in shock and did not say anything nor did they see the huge man that passed by them. They were relieved to be out of the water but couldn't figure out what was happening and how.

Flying back was taking longer with more bodies holding onto her and keeping her from staying high above the water. She pulled the children onto her back and kept the parents at her sides as she held onto them.

"Stay close to me and hold on as tightly as you can. We are almost at the island now. I will take you to a hut where you can stay until the storm passes. You will be safe there."

The family only nodded and looked startled by everything that was happening to them. They wondered if they were dreaming.

Branyrd was relieved to get back to Candle Island and get the family safely inside out of the storm. They didn't want to let her go at first for fear they would fall.

"You are safe now. Get dry and eat something. These people will help you. I will be back after we get the rest of the people out of the water."

"I don't know what just happened to us. I can't even think straight right now. I think we are all still in shock. How could this happen? Who are you? Where did you come from?" the man asked as his family looked on with dazed expressions.

Branyrd stated in a calm voice, "I have been sent here to help you all. That is all you need to know for now. I will be back to check on you."

The other natives hovered over the new arrivals and gave them some food and drink and told them, "It is difficult to understand what just happened to you. We are thankful you are okay and didn't drown. Branyrd is an Angel. That is why she can do these things."

"I...I have never seen an Angel before," the little boy announced with wide eyes.

"I never did either," his sister said in wonder.

"We had never seen an Angel before either," one woman said. "We would all have died if it had not been for these two Angels."

"Two Angels?" another man questioned.

"Yes, did you not see the big man yet? He is helping Branyrd. His name is Benedicto," one native said.

"They have been here to help us through this storm and also to rebuild these huts and buildings that were once destroyed," another native explained.

"Oh, I think you mean by us, don't you?" the father said, looking ashamed. "We did not want to harm anyone. It was our ruler."

"Yes, we know all that. Your ruler and ours are here in another building staying out of the storm. I am sure they will come to an agreement about what must be done for all of us to live in peace."

"Where is the Angel now, Daddy?" the boy asked.

"I think she will come back. She said she would."

"Are we safe now, Daddy?" his daughter asked with frightened eyes.

"Yes, I think we are, honey. Why don't you and your brother find a place to lay down and rest. Okay?"

The man shivered when he thought over what could have been. He was thankful but didn't understand any of this about Angels.

The children were given blankets to wrap in and soon fell asleep.

CHAPTER EIGHTEEN

Benedicto had lifted the rest of the people out of the water by the time Branyrd had flown back to help.

"Everything is fine now, Angel. Help me get these people into another hut. I am going back to look over the area around the island to make sure we didn't miss anyone."

"Okay. I will come back shortly to assist you."

Branyrd hurried back and got everyone settled in another hut. Once she was satisfied that they were all comfortable and taken care of by the others, she flew back to the sinking island to find Benedicto.

She whispered her Guardian Angel's name and waited. She couldn't see him in the rising smoke and feared he was lost in it. She knew that he was an Angel and protected by HIM but still she called out to Benedicto.

Branyrd kept flying back and forth and all around the island to find him. Benedicto was nowhere in sight. She looked up to Heaven and prayed for guidance. *What was she going to do if she couldn't find her Guardian Angel?*

Suddenly she heard a cry and looked down. There on the shore was a little girl inches from the smoke and heat that would soon touch her.

Branyrd didn't stop to think, she flew down and grabbed the little girl who was now unconscious and burned by the heat. She dipped her into the cooler water and bathed her burns on her legs. The cool water revived the little girl and she opened her eyes to see the Angel.

"Who are you? Where is my mommy and daddy?"

"Were they with you?" Branyrd asked in a soft voice to calm the girl.

"I think so. I don't know where they went? How did I get up in the air? Can you fly?"

"Yes, I can fly. What is your name?"

"I am Amara and I am six years old. My legs hurt!"

"I know, sweet pea. I will try to take the pain away. Let me dip you in the cool water again. Okay?"

"Okay. It does feel a little better. Thank you. Will you find my mommy and daddy now?"

"Yes, I am looking for them. Maybe they went into the water. They must be worried about you too." Branyrd concentrated on the shoreline and further out. There was no sign of anyone else around.

"Angel, are you all right?" Benedicto appeared beside her with a concerned expression his face.

"Yes, I'm fine but this little girl is not. We need to take care of her burns. Can you keep a lookout for her parents? She said they were with her but I can't find them."

"They could have gotten in the water and pulled with the tide in that direction." Benedicto pointed and headed that way. "I will see if I can find them over there. Take the little girl back and put some of the aloe plant on her burns right away. The natives will know what to do to help her."

"Yes, I was planning on doing that. I will be back again to help you find them," Branyrd said as she flew back to Candle Island once again.

"Wow, you can fly fast!" the little girl exclaimed as she put her hands out to try to fly too.

"Don't let go of me, Amara. I don't want to lose you."

"Okay. I hope you find my mommy and daddy so I can tell them that I can fly." Amara smiled but then grimaced when a stab of pain came back to remind her that she was injured.

"Don't worry. I will put some medicine on your burns and make you feel better soon. Okay?"

"Okay," Amara said through the tears that kept flooding her eyes. "It really hurts now! Ow!"

"Okay, sweet pea. We are almost there now. Hold on a little longer."

When Branyrd down looked at Amara, she had passed out again. "Poor thing, she sighed. "We must get you better. Please help me, LORD!"

As soon as Branyrd's feet touched the shore she raced with Amara to the hut of Mortan and Miriam. She believed that they would be able to take care of the little girl until she could find the parents.

The old couple opened the door and looked at the bundle in Branyrd's arms. "What happened to this child?" Miriam asked as she put her arms out to take the little girl inside.

"She has been badly burned on her legs. I will leave her in your care while I go back to find her parents."

"Poor child," Mortan said. "Give her to me. I have some aloe that will help her."

"Yes, we need to get some of the Kava plant to stop the pain. She is suffering. Look at her, even though she is unconscious, she can still feel the pain."

The old couple mixed some of the different plants together and made a poultice and a brew of Chamomile to calm the child down. When Amara opened her eyes, she smiled at the couple. "Are you taking care of me? Thank you. My legs feel better now. Where are my mommy and daddy?"

"Don't worry, little one. Branyrd is going to find them. Why don't you drink some of this tea and rest. When you wake up again, they will be here."

"You don't know that," Mortan whispered to his wife. "You can't promise her that. What if they are…"

"Don't think it for it could be true. Branyrd will find them. I know she will. She is an Angel," Miriam retorted.

***

Benedicto was joined by Branyrd as they combed the beach and further out into the water following the currents. There was no sign of anyone.

Branyrd shook her head and couldn't stop the tears as she cried out, "LORD, you can't take Amara's parents. She is just a child. She needs them. Please help us find them!"

CHAPTER NINETEEN

Benedicto and Branyrd came back to the huts as the rain and wind were lessening now. They went from hut to hut to ensure that everyone was doing well. They visited the hut of Mortan and Miriam to check on Amara.

"How is she doing?" Branyrd asked as she touched the child's forehead saying a prayer for her recovery.

"She is doing better. The aloe and Kava along with the Chamomile worked to calm her down so she could sleep."

"That's good to hear," Branyrd sighed.

Mortan hesitated but asked, "Did you find her parents?"

"No, we could not find anyone else in the water. We fear they may have been taken by the currents."

"Oh no. That is unthinkable. What are we going to tell her?" Miriam asked with tears in her eyes.

"Nothing right now. We will keep her safe and sedated as best we can with the medicinal plants," Branyrd took the woman's hands and held them tightly. "Let's wait and see how she is."

"We will take care of her. We never had any children of our own. We can be her grandparents though since we are so old now," Miriam said with a wane smile.

"Yes, we will take care of her as if she were our own," Mortan said with a choked voice as he lovingly touched Amara's long black hair.

***

In another hut a couple cried out in agony over the loss of their young daughter. They had looked around them one minute and then the next she was gone. They feared that she had drowned.

Many others in the hut with them tried to console the couple to no avail. The mother cried out calling her daughter's name, "Amara, where are you? Oh god of love and mercy, you cannot take her from us. Please help us."

One of the others who had been rescued by the Angels spoke up, "Maybe you should let one of the Angels pray for your daughter. Their god seems to listen to them more than ours does."

"What do you mean?' the bereaved mother asked.

"Well, since the two of them have been here on our island we have experienced many miracles and heard of others on the other islands that they visited."

"What miracles?" the father asked as he looked at his wife in disbelief.

"Look what they did for us. They built these huts and other buildings all over the area where everything was once destroyed by your people," one person explained.

"I didn't realize that our people destroyed anything. They said they were checking over the neighboring islands to see which one would be the best suited for our new home."

"No, that is not what they did!" a man exclaimed, anger evident in his eyes and manner.

"Oh, I'm sorry. We did not know that. None of the people knew that. We never would have allowed that to happen if we knew." Tears were evident in the couple's eyes even more so now.

"Did you lose your home?"

"Yes, and my husband too," one woman yelled out.

"Me too," another roared back in anger.

"How did they do this and why?" the tearful woman asked.

"Because they needed a new home and this island was full of natives who were living peacefully here, that is why! They did not think of what pain and suffering they would cause us."

The woman put her arms around this last person to say this. "I apologize for what our people did to you and your islanders. How can we stay here now knowing how you feel about us?"

"I don't know," the woman replied as she moved away from the bereaving mother.

The couple got up and left the hut to sit on the beach where the rain had now subsided but the wind was still brisk. They watched the wind blow across the water causing caps to form and closed their eyes as the tears kept coming.

What were they going to do without their daughter and now stranded in a place where they were not wanted?

The husband wrapped his wife in his arms and let her cry on his shoulder. He let his tears fall for the devastating loss that they would never be able to forget.

***

Branyrd and Benedicto finished visiting all the huts to check on everyone. They noticed the lone couple sitting on the beach staring into the water wrapped in one another's arms.

"What do you think is wrong here? Do you think they miss their former home or is it something else?" Branyrd whispered.

"I don't know but we could ask them if they need help in some way." Benedicto headed down the beach to stand next to the couple.

"Excuse me. I am Benedicto and this is Branyrd." The Angel stood next to him and looked at the emotional couple.

"Can we help you in some way? Are you injured?" Branyrd asked as she knelt next to them.

"No. We are fine. We are grieving our loss right now," the woman replied through tears.

Branyrd felt their profound sadness as she asked, "Oh, I'm sorry. Did you lose someone on the island?"

"Yes," the man answered when his wife was too emotional to speak "We lost our young daughter."

"Oh," Branyrd couldn't get her breath as she began to think about Amara.

"What is her name?" the Angel inquired in a soft, calm voice.

"Amara. She is only six years old. She was with us one minute when we went into the water then she disappeared. I tried to hold onto her hand but she let go and we were swept out into the current where you picked us up."

"Yes, I remember helping you," Branyrd said in a hushed voice.

The Angel exchanged smiles with Benedicto before continuing, "Maybe we can help you find Amara."

Mother and father looked at her in shock. "How would you do that? Do you know where she is?"

CHAPTER TWENTY

Inside the old couple's hut Amara woke up screaming in pain once again. She called out, "Mommy, Daddy where are you?"

The man gently put more aloe on the girl's legs while his wife gave her more Chamomile tea to calm her along with some Kava to ease the pain.

A knock was heard at their door and before they could open it, Branyrd and Benedicto were there with another couple.

Amara sat up with a groan as she heard a familiar voice. "Amara, oh my god, you are alive!" the mother said as she cried tears of relief.

"Mommy, Daddy! I was calling you. Where did you go?"

"We are here now, Amara, and will never leave your side again," the father said as he hugged his daughter gently and appraised the burns she had on her legs.

"Oh, my sweetheart! Your legs must hurt you so much! I'm so sorry we got separated in the water. We looked everywhere for you but thought we had lost you," he said.

"We are here now, Amara. You will get better. We will make sure of it," her mother exclaimed as she held onto her daughter as she kissed her face and touched her hair to assure herself that her daughter was alive.

Branyrd cleared her throat and interrupted the happy family, "I found Amara on the shore. She had not gone far into the water. Somehow, she was tossed back to shore where she got too close to the heat from the lava and received those burns. We brought here to this hut where this couple have been taking care of her."

"Oh, my goodness, thank you, Branyrd, and thank you too," the mother said as she took the couple's hands into her own and held them tightly in gratitude. "We appreciate your caring for Amara. She must have been so frightened to be alone without us. I can't thank you enough."

The father shook their hands and reiterated the same thanks to them.

Amara watched as her parents spoke to the old people. "Mommy and Daddy. This nice lady and man are going to be my grandparents. I heard them say that. They don't have any children of their own. I want them to be my Mimi and Papa. I don't have any grandparents now. They were on the island and didn't get off. Right?"

"Yes, that is correct, Amara. They are…"

Before the mother could continue the old couple came over and put their arms around her and said, "We are here for Amara if you want us to be her Mimi and Papa."

"If Amara wants that then that is what you will be. Welcome to the family," the father announced with a smile and a wink to his daughter.

"Hurray, ow!" Amara said as her movements caused her pain to return and the tears ran once again.

"It's okay, dushi," the old couple retorted as they cuddled the little girl in their arms one on each side of her.

Amara smiled and gave her new grandparents a kiss on their cheeks, much to their surprise and delight. She said, "What is dushi?"

"That means sweetheart. You are our little dushi."

"Oh, I like that. Mommy and Daddy, I am Mimi's and Papa's little dushi!"

The couples broke out in giggles which made Amara smile widely because giggling would have hurt too much.

Amara laid back and fell asleep once again after finishing up the Kava and Chamomile tea.

Branyrd and Benedicto left the hut after seeing all was well with the couples and everyone was getting along. Now it was time to call everyone out to speak with them. Maybe they would all get along soon too after talking it all out.

Branyrd grimaced when she heard yelling coming from the hut with the rulers. It didn't sound too peaceful there.'

CHAPTER TWENTY-ONE

"What do you mean you are now in control of Candle Island?" Kamalnayo shrieked in a pitched voice.

"Yes, most of the people here are my people from Wanalami. You have the other islands to command. This will be mine."

"No, absolutely not! I am ruler of all the archipelago. I have been here since my father's father and before," Kamalnayo responded.

"But you cannot be in all places at one time. We need to work together," Marnolani demanded.

"Wait a minute!" Branyrd stepped between them before fists or swords would fly back and forth in anger.

"You can both rule the island together in peace. You need to let your people know that they are safe and well cared for here by both of you. Two rulers are better than no ruler. Wouldn't you say?" Branyrd watched the eyes of the rulers as they stared at each other, neither giving in.

Benedicto laughed his full-bodied laugh that caught the attention of both rulers.

"Why are you laughing, giant?" Marnolani asked.

"He is my friend, Marnolani. Do not address Benedicto in that manner. It is rude. Don't you know that he is a powerful magic man?"

"What do you mean, Kamalnayo? What magic can he do?"

"He made a pineapple out of thin air and gave it to me. It was the sweetest and tastiest pineapple I ever had." Kamalnayo put his arm around Benedicto in solidarity.

"Show me this magic, Benedicto. I want to taste the sweetest pineapple," Marnolani begged.

"He also brought my son back from the dead. Who of your people can do that, Marnolani?" Kamalnayo inquired with a smirk.

"Oh, I…I don't have a medicine man anymore. He perished in the lava. I saw him disappear right before my eyes. I never want to see that again. I need a medicine man on my island here. Will you be my medicine man, Benedicto?" Marnolani beseeched.

"No, I cannot, Marnolani. I am not staying here for long. I will be leaving shortly to go back to my own place."

"Where is that, Benedicto?" Marnolani asked as he frowned in disappointment.

"It is far from here."

Branyrd interrupted before the ruler asked another question, "We are here to help you get the island back in one piece and the people situated and happy again. There is much to be done yet. You cannot keep squabbling like this in front of your people. What would they think of you both? You must show them strength and courage now."

"Yes, I agree with Branyrd. She is a magical person too. She is the one who built all these huts and buildings to house all of us in such a short time before the storm. If she had not done that, we would all have perished." Kamalnayo nodded and smiled at Branyrd.

Branyrd nodded back and said, "That is exactly what we need to do now. There is much more building to do to get the people situated before another storm comes this way. These huts were for temporary use but they will need to be reinforced again since they were buffeted by the rain and wind. Everyone has a job to do but you rulers must organize them to do the jobs."

Kamalnayo stepped forward and called out to the people in a commanding voice, "Come out of your huts, Candlerians and Wanalamians to rebuild your island!"

"Yes, all of us are now Candlerians. This is our island for all to live in peace and prosperity. We must work together," Marnolani said in agreement with Kamalnayo as they exchanged knowing looks and smiled.

The people rushed out of the huts and listened to the two rulers who shared the role of co-rulers. They each had something to tell their people about what they expected them to do.

All the natives rushed to-and-fro to gather wood and clear the beach of palm trees, leaves, and anything else that had been swept there by the high winds and rain. In no time the beach was cleared and the extra wood from the trees was being used to build more places for storage of supplies that would be coming from the other islands per Kamalnayo.

Kamalnayo directed several of the men to come with him to the Peeples Island to gather more supplies, food and clothes for all the people. He pulled one of the boats with the men's help into the water and several more natives did the same with the other boats. Soon they were off rowing back to the other islands.

The rest of the men and women gathered to decide where they wanted to put the supply huts and how many they would need.

Benedicto and Branyrd watched as things were looking better between the islanders. They were getting along for now with a task that kept them busy. What would happen when they were all done with their rebuilding?

The children raced around and chased one another without a care in the world. It was as if there never was a sinking island, a terrible storm or loss of lives. They were innocents who knew nothing but love and laughter in the calm of things. This made Branyrd smile and laugh along with them as she watched Misty chase after them, barking happily.

Amara sat on the beach with her parents and Mimi and Papa watching over her. Amara sighed, "I wish I could run and play with the other children. How long will I have to rest my legs and when will the pain go away for good?"

Branyrd heard Amara's remark and felt sad for her. "Why can't I help heal her, LORD? No child should suffer like she is suffering."

"Yes, I agree, Branyrd. Go to her and lay your hands over her legs and pray. She will soon be well enough to run and play like the others."

"Thank you, LORD."

Branyrd went quickly to the little girl's aid and did what she was told by the LORD. Amara smiled at Branyrd and said, "What are you doing to my legs, Branyrd? They are tingling!"

"Are they hurting you?" Branyrd enquired.

"No, they are tickling me but not hurting anymore. Did you make me all better, Angel?"

"Do you feel better, Amara?"

"Yes, I do! How did you do that, Branyrd?" Amara's innocent smile was glowing with good health now.

"I did not do that. It was HIM, Amara. Remember I told you to pray and you would feel better soon?"

"You did? I don't remember. I guess I must have fallen asleep."

"Oh, I see. But now you know what to do if you feel sick again. Okay?

"Yes, but what do I say to HIM?"

"Well, you tell HIM your problems and HE will do what HE thinks needs to be done."

"Okay. I guess I can do that. Can I go play now with the others?"

"Yes, you can, Amara. Have fun." Branyrd smiled as she watched Amara run as fast as she could on her healed legs.

"Oh, my goodness! You healed our daughter, Branyrd!" the parents exclaimed in joy.

"HE did it, not I."

"What do you mean, Branyrd?"

She explained to the parents as she did to Amara.

"But everyone said that you are an Angel. Angels can do all sorts of things. Right?"

"We can only do what HE allows us to do and with HIS help."

"Our god does not listen to us. We prayed for him to find our daughter but he didn't, you did. I think we will pray from now on to yours. HE works faster and does a better job of things."

Branyrd giggled at their words but said, "We all want to believe in our own way that things will work out the way we want. They don't always. But you must never lose faith and believe that all things are possible."

"Yes, I think we do believe now that all things are possible after what we have seen you do to help us and our new home recover. Thank you."

"It is my pleasure. After all, this has been my mission to do everything in my power to help you get back on your feet and restore your homes. We are not through yet and will not leave until you are all settled and things get back to normal."

"That's good to hear, Branyrd. But why don't you stay here with us? This can be your home and Benedicto's too. Don't you like it here?"

"Oh, yes, it is a paradise but different from the paradise we come from. But it is beautiful. We have another mission to complete elsewhere. HE has plans for us when we return."

"Okay. But we will miss you both. You have done so much to help us. We couldn't have done any of it without your help."

Before Branyrd could say anything else she heard a frantic barking and Misty heading their way with frightened eyes.

CHAPTER TWENTY-TWO

"What's wrong, Misty?" Branyrd bent close to the dog to hear his thoughts.

Misty met Branyrd's eyes as he barked a few more times and turned to looked back the way he came, in alarm. He stomped his feet and jumped up and down trying to tell the adults there was a problem.

Benedicto and Branyrd listened to Misty's thoughts then ran after him to where the children were gathered, transfixed and afraid to move as they glanced downward.

The Angels looked at the feet of the children and saw a bomb that was live. There was another one close by. They whispered in alarm to each other sharing their thoughts of what they must do. "We can't let them move. We need to get the children out of there without the bombs going off."

The adults had followed the Angels to see what the problem was and stopped when they saw Benedicto raise his hands to them. "Don't go any further. There is a bomb or bombs here. The children are trapped in the middle of them. We cannot risk having anyone else get too close or the bombs will go off."

"Oh no!" Amara's parents and others cried out in alarm. "Please protect them!"

The Sisters of Love hurried over to call out to the children. "Stay still. Don't move. Let the Angels take care of you. You will be safe, the LORD willing. Don't be frightened."

The children, hearing this, began to cry and hold onto one another. Misty barked at them to stay there. He was the one who had warned them not to move. When the children saw the bombs, they stopped in time.

"You will be all right, Amara. Don't move, sweetheart. Stay very still. Let Branyrd and Benedicto take care of the bombs and get them out of the way," her parents stated calmly but their voices shook with fright.

"Dushi, we love you. Stay quiet and still, little one," her adopted Mimi and Papa cried out as they wiped tears away and held onto one another. Terror was visible in their eyes over the idea of losing their newly adopted granddaughter.

The natives started praying to their god and HIM both to make sure that someone would hear them and come to their rescue.

The rulers came alongside the Angels and conferred. "What are you going to do to keep the children safe? How can you pick up a bomb without it going off?" Kamalnayo asked.

"That is the problem we plan to solve, Kamalnayo. We will do it but need to ask for HIS assistance in keeping the children safe."

"Do you want us to pray with you?" other natives asked. "We have been praying to our gods and yours, hoping one would answer our prayers."

"I'm sure HE has heard your prayers. Now we wait until HE tells us what we can do."

"When will HE tell you what to do, Branyrd?" Amara's mother asked with wide-eyes filled with tears.

"Don't worry, we will know soon. Be patient and keep praying. HE loves to hear from everyone."

A little voice was heard in the distance followed by another. "Where are you? We are here waiting for you." It was Seth, Freya and Dack. There were off in the distance and waving at everyone. "What are you doing over there?"

Branyrd lifted her feet off the ground and swiftly flew over and landed next to the three children to tell them what was happening. "Don't move forward or backward. There are bombs in this field. The other children are trapped over there. You were lucky that you didn't step on one of them."

"We ran around the field to hide from the rest of them. But they ran through the field and then stopped when Misty began to bark. We kept calling Misty but he ran the other way. What do we do now? Can we go back there with the others?"

"No. You must stay right here. I will stay with you until we figure out what we will do."

"Will any of my friends die from the bombs?" Seth asked in a quivering voice.

"No, we will get them out but it will take a little time to do that. If you want to go back to your parents, I will fly you back there."

"Yes, Branyrd!" Seth yelled first. "Take me first. I love to fly! I didn't get to fly like some of the others that were on the sinking island. They told us about that."

"Okay, but you must hold on tight, all three of you. I can take all of you together. Please hold on tight and off we go!"

The children whooped and hollered in delight as they flew with Branyrd. She held onto them and placed them on the ground far from the field and into their parent's and others' arms.

"I loved that, Branyrd! Can we do it again some time?" Seth asked with wide-eyed wonder.

"We'll see, Seth. Right now, I must help Benedicto get the other children away safely."

"Okay. I don't want any of my new friends to die."

"I won't let them, Seth. Don't worry. Stay with your sister and parents now. You too, Dack. Go to the sisters. They will watch over you."

"No, I want to stay with Seth and Freya. They are my friends. I want them to be my family."

"Oh, okay." Branyrd looked over at Seth and Freya's parents who shrugged their shoulders and nodded. "It's okay. He can stay with us. He has become like one of the family," the mother said as she patted Dack's head along with her own children's and held them close.

Branyrd and Benedicto prayed and conferred with one another after receiving word from the LORD what they must do.

Everyone held their breaths as they watched Branyrd hover over the trapped children and reach down to pick one at a time up and away from the bomb. She swiftly flew with a few children in her arms and brought them over to the sisters and parents who were waiting to take them away from there.

Benedicto picked up more children and smoothly flew them to the sisters. The two Angels kept doing this until they had all the children safely away from the bombs.

They told all the mothers and babies, natives, sisters, and children, "You must move away as fast as you can back to your huts. We will be detonating the bombs and do not want anyone around when we do that."

Everyone raced away, running and tripping over one another in their haste, children screaming and parents holding onto them as they were afraid to look back.

"Please be careful," Sister Superior said to her charges. "Don't push and shove. We will get away safely."

Amara was led away with her parents and adopted grandparents who were relieved that she was now safe.

Seth, Freya and Dack held onto another and followed the others with their parents' urging. "Watch where you are going and head back to our hut. We will be safe there, children," their father said in a calm voice.

He and his wife exchanged worried glances but tried to keep calm themselves so they children would not worry.

"Will the Angels be okay, Daddy?" Seth asked with fear in his eyes.

"Yes, their god will help them," he smiled to hide his own fear.

"Why don't you three go inside the hut and find something to do until this is all settled. Okay?" their mother announced as she ushered them into the hut for safety.

The other natives and sisters were doing the same thing. They were all hiding out in their huts and praying that the Angels would survive.

CHAPTER TWENTY-THREE

Branyrd and Benedicto carefully lifted one bomb and flew into the air as fast as they could and then tossed it into the water far from the islands.

The bomb didn't explode right away but floated to the surface and sat there.

"Look at that, Benedicto! It didn't explode after all," Branyrd announced in surprise.

"I think it will eventually. Just wait a minute," Benedicto said as he smirked at her and covered his ears.

"What? How do you know that?" Branyrd asked as she gave him a stern expression that always messed up her angelic face.

"Oh boy, there's that quirky face again, Angel!" Benedicto laughed.

"Why are you covering your ears. It didn't explode," Branyrd announced, but no sooner were her words spoken that a massive explosion was heard and fish were tossed up in the air.

"What happened?" she asked in shock as her ears were ringing from the sound.

"I told you wait a minute," Benedicto guffawed.

"Well, you could have warned me to cover my ears too," Branyrd expressed her displeasure.

"Did you not see me covering mine, Angel?"

"Um, yes, I did. But I thought you were trying to be funny."

"We are not through yet. We have a couple more to lift out. Be careful. We may not be as lucky. They could explode sooner."

"Are you kidding me? Wouldn't HE keep us safe from that?"

"Yes, HE can, but will HE?"

"Stop this right now, Benedicto! I don't believe you sometimes. You don't appear to be an Angel. You really are a tease and enjoy tormenting me."

"No, I do not, Angel. I am trying to ease the tension you are feeling at this moment. Was I successful?"

"No, not at all! Let's get this over with! I don't think my human feelings can take any more of your mischievous nature."

"Are you angry with me, Angel? You know I would never hurt you intentionally with my teasing. It is my way of dealing with difficult situations and easing tension for you."

"Okay. I forgive you, Benedicto. I know you are a kind Guardian Angel and would never hurt me on purpose. I guess I am being too human and emotional right now. It is frightening to think that one of these children or more could have been killed by these bombs. Let's take care of the rest of them and make a sweep over the rest of the island before we let them move about."

"That is my intention, Angel. Let's do it!"

The Angels pulled up another bomb and moved further away from the islands to drop it. Fish were tossed once again this time sooner than before. The Angels managed to move away before that happened and this time Branyrd had her ears covered.

"There's another one over here, Branyrd. Let's get it out and fly even further away. We don't want to disturb all the fish in one area. There will be plenty floating around for the larger fish to consume. These fish may attract some sharks too."

Branyrd looked over at the huts and saw the children peeking out at them. She waved at them to stay there.

Seth stepped out with Dack and continued to watch the Angels work to get the last bomb out of the area. "Better cover your ears, Dack. The last one was louder than the first!"

"I know. My ears are still ringing. Are yours?"

"Yes. I can barely hear you," Seth said as he shook his head to try to stop the ringing.

"Look at the water, Seth! There are a lot of fish floating there."

"I see them. I guess the bomb killed them. That could have been one of us instead."

"I know. I get the creeps about that. I hope the Angels get all the bombs so we can go out and play again."

"I agree, Dack. I don't like staying inside. It's no fun. There isn't anything to do."

"We will have plenty of fish to eat for dinner tonight," Seth said with a giggle.

He looked up again as the Angels flew away with another bomb. "Where are they going?"

"I think they are going to toss it out into the water farther away from here," Dack said.

"I think you're right, Dack. Look they are still flying past the other island that is on fire. Maybe they are going to drop it on top of it to stop the volcano."

"That would be cool if they could stop the fire. Maybe the island wouldn't sink after all."

"It still would not be safe to go there though. The people who came from there will have to stay with us forever," Seth stated.

"That's okay. We already made friends with some of the children. There aren't too many of us left here so we needed to have some more people."

"I guess so, Dack. It's nice to have more friends. I'm glad I met you. You are my best friend now. Right?"

"Yep, and maybe I will be like a brother to you and Freya. I don't have any other family. Do you think your parents will adopt me?"

"I'll ask them. I will tell them that I need a brother," Seth announced with a smile.

"Look, the bomb just went off but we didn't hear it. It must really be far away. I just saw the water splashing and fish flying up."

"I hope there are some fish left in the ocean though, Dack."

"There are some larger fish eating them here. Do you see them? They must be sharks."

"Oh my! Yes, I see them. We can't go in the water until they go away, Dack."

Some of the others came out to see what the two boys were looking at in the water.

"Sharks! There are sharks here!" one islander yelled.

"There are never sharks this close to the shore. They always go out farther to feed," another native said.

"Keep away from the water, boys. It is not safe right now. Let them finish up feeding and clearing out the dead fish. We wouldn't be able to eat them anyway. They could be tainted from the bombs," someone else announced.

The Angels flew back to the beach and gathered the people together outside the huts. "We are not through with the bombs. We suspect there may be more spread around the island. We will be flying over and checking out the area.

Please stay close to the huts until we return. It may not be safe," Branyrd announced and set off again with Benedicto before anyone else could respond.

CHAPTER TWENTY-FOUR

Seth sat with his sister and parents after the Angel left and asked, "Will you adopt Dack? We are best friends now. I really need a brother. I can be his big brother because I am seven and he is six."

"Hmm. That is funny because we were just discussing that, Seth," his father said.

Seth looked at his parents with eager anticipation.

"We have decided, if you all agree, that we would love to make Dack part of our family," his mother announced with a broad smile.

"Hurray! Did you hear that Dack? We are going to be brothers!"

"Yay!" Dack yelled as he jumped around while hugging Seth.

"Aren't you happy, Freya?" Seth asked as his sister sat in the corner looking sad.

"Don't you like me, Freya?" Dack asked with a frown.

"Of course, I like you, Dack. I just feel left out. I wish I could have a sister."

"Well, a brother is just as good, Freya. Now there are two brothers to play with and watch over," Seth announced with a smile as he hugged her.

Dack came along and hugged his new sister too and gave her a kiss on the cheek, much to her surprise.

"I guess, it's okay," she smiled back at both and hugged them tight.

Their parents sighed in relief and announced, "Well, now that we are going to be one big happy family, we need to give everyone a job to do."

"Aww, Mom! Do we have to do chores now?" Seth whined.

"Well, yes, you do, Seth, Dack and Freya. If you want to eat dinner. I need for you to help me pick some palm leaves around the hut so we can make a basket. Once the Angels say it is safe, we will go further out and pick some coconuts and fruit to carry back here."

"Okay," the three children chorused and giggled when they saw their mother's face break out in a snicker.

***

On the other side of the island the Angels scoured the land and spotted more bombs that had not exploded. They dipped down and retrieved them one at a time and flew away to deposit them in the ocean.

"I hope we don't find too many more or there will not be any fish left in the ocean," Branyrd sighed.

"Not to worry, Angel. HE will take care of that. The sharks are doing a good job cleaning up the dead ones."

After all the bombs had exploded in the ocean and the dead fish were mostly consumed by the sharks and other large fish, the Angels went back to the beach to see the islanders and called them to a meeting.

"We have taken care of all the bombs on the island. It is now safe to move around. Please stay away from the water for a little while longer. There may still be sharks out there feasting on the dead fish," Branyrd announced.

"Can we go out to pick some fruit now, Branyrd?" Seth asked as he looked at his parents for their approval too.

"Yes, it is safe but go with an adult for the time being. I don't want anyone roaming around without someone along in case you need help."

"Why would we need help, Branyrd?" Seth's father asked.

"Well, we are sure we got every bomb but I don't want anyone stepping on something that is sharp because of all the debris that is still scattered around. That is a job that you must all tackle when you finish cleaning up the village and live there again."

"I see. Yes, you are right, Branyrd. We still have much to do to get our homes in order and the village back to where we can live in safety," Seth's father stated.

"You have done so much for us. How can we ever repay you both?" one native asked.

"There is no need to repay us for anything we have done. We did this because we wanted to help you get your lives back together. HE wanted us to do this because HE loves everyone here."

"HE does?" one woman asked in disbelief.

"How does HE know us?" a man asked.

"Well, like I have told many of you. HE knows every one of you because HE is the one who put you here."

The Angels looked around at the confusion on the islanders' faces.

"Do you love one another?" Benedicto asked.

"What do you mean?" one islander asked.

"Well, do you love your family, your neighbors?"

"Yes, we love our families but we don't know some of the new people here yet."

"Well, in time you will get to know them and love them like your own family. Why, you ask? Because you will come to depend upon one another to survive," Branyrd added.

"Oh, I see. We will need one another in order to get everything back in order like you have been doing for us," another woman said in response.

"Does that mean that you are leaving us, Branyrd and Benedicto?" Seth asked, worry lining his face.

"Eventually we will be leaving to go on another mission to help others as HE requests," Branyrd answered.

"Oh, do other people need you like we did?" Dack asked.

"Yes, there are many who need our help just like you did. Once we help those in need we leave and go to help others," Benedicto stated.

"Will you come back again and visit us?" Freya asked in a timid voice.

"No, I'm sorry we cannot do that, Freya," Branyrd stated with a sad sigh. "We will keep you always in our hearts and memories."

"We will always remember you too, Branyrd and Benedicto," Seth said with tears in his eyes.

"Don't cry, Seth. You will grow up one day and forget all about us," Branyrd responded with a wistful smile.

"Well, I don't know about that. You will be hard to forget," he answered with a forced smile.

"That's nice to hear, Seth. I will never forget you or anyone else here either!"

"Thank you," Seth said as he gripped Branyrd in a tight hug and sniffled his tears away.

Branyrd patted his head and hugged him back and said, "It's okay, Seth. You will be fine without us. You have your family to take care of you."

"Oh, yes, I almost forgot to tell you! I have a new brother!"

"You do?" Branyrd looked at Seth's parents and they nodded.

"Yes, Dack is going to be my brother from now on. He is my best friend too!" Seth announced with a giggle.

"Wow! That's wonderful to hear, Seth." Branyrd patted him on the head and felt her own tears brimming.

Seth looked at the Angel. "Are you going to cry too, Branyrd? Did I make you unhappy?"

"Oh no, of course not, Seth. These are tears of joy for you and your family."

"Okay. I didn't want to make you cry. That wouldn't be a nice thing to do to an Angel."

"It's okay, Seth. I'm fine. I am happy for you, Dack and your sister. Now you have each other to love and take care of and do all kinds of family things together."

"Yes, I can't wait until we get settled in our new homes. Now we need to help my mother make a new basket and then get dinner ready. She said we have to pick some coconuts and fruit."

"Well, you better go and help her." Branyrd watched Seth run along to help his brother and sister make a basket. She sighed and wiped the tears away.

"Are you okay, Angel?" Benedicto looked at her and caught a tear that escaped.

"I'm fine. You know me. It's just my human emotions bursting out all over again. I know we will be leaving soon and I find it so difficult to do each time. I feel a strong affinity to everyone here. They are special people, so

150

resilient and strong. I have never seen any others like them. They have suffered so much and still can smile and be happy."

"Yes, humans are like that. Not all of them are as strong though. But when they must be, they find the strength in themselves that HE provides."

"What are we going to do now for them? They look as if they don't need us anymore."

"We are not ready to leave. HE has not given us the signal to leave. When HE thinks we are done here, HE will tell us."

There was a noise coming from one of the huts as the door burst open and a person fell out or rather was pushed out.

CHAPTER TWENTY-FIVE

Kamalnayo came out of the hut and looked down at the man who was on the ground where he had pushed him.

"Who do you think you are?" he yelled at the man.

"I am the ruler of Wanalami and now co-ruler of this island," the man responded.

"No, you are not! I am the ruler of all these islands and you are one of its inhabitants. That is all," Kamalnayo exclaimed with vehemence.

Marnolani answered in a strong voice, "I am not just a native here. You should show me some respect as only a ruler deserves."

"Why should I?"

"You need me to speak to my people so that they will help you get this island back to a livable place. They will not listen to you, Kamalnayo. You are not their leader."

"They will listen or I will send them back to Wanalami."

"You cannot do that! It is destroyed and unlivable. We must all live together now and get along. You have no other choice but to comply. We have nowhere to go unless you want us to go to one of the other islands."

"No, I control all Peeples Islands. You will stay here until I can come up with a solution to this problem. In the meantime, you will do as I say and so will your people."

Marnolani got up and brushed off his cloak of sand and stormed away. Two men followed closely behind him as they went toward the village to get away from Kamalnayo until he came to his senses. The two men were Marnolani's guards and always stayed close to him in case they were needed.

Once they reached the village where some of the buildings were being rebuilt, they found a place to sit and talk about what they would do next.

One guard asked, "What do you want us to do? Shall we kill Kamalnayo so you can become ruler?"

"What? Don't talk nonsense. He is important to his people and they will rebel against me. No, we will wait until he needs us."

"Shall we tell the rest of your people not to listen to him?"

"No, just wait. Time will lead him to me soon enough."

The two men exchanged confused expressions and shrugged their shoulders.

"Go back to the others. I need to be alone to think."

"Yes, Marnolani. We will do that right away."

Once the ruler was alone, he sighed and looked around. There was still much to do to make this island inhabitable again. He felt great loss for those that had lost their homes and family. He knew it had been his fault even if he hadn't dropped the bombs himself. He also knew that Kamalnayo could not do it alone without his help and the help of his people. What he couldn't do was share how he was involved and who was behind the island's destruction. There was much restitution on his part to complete.

***

Branyrd and Benedicto hovered close by to listen in on the conversation of Marnolani and his men. They were not sure that the disagreements between these two rulers were finished. There was more trouble coming. They would have to stay close to Kamalnayo to ensure his safety from harm and keep the people busy rebuilding their village and strengthening the bond amongst them.

The Angel went back to see Kamalnayo and see how she could help him get his island back to normal.

"Are you looking for me, Branyrd?" Kamalnayo stepped out of his hut and stopped in front of the Angel.

"Yes, I was. Are you okay now?"

"Yes, why shouldn't I be? That imbecile, Marnolani, should be shipped out to another island along with his people. If I could do that I would. He is nothing but trouble for all of us. He is the one responsible for my island being in shambles and my people mourning their losses."

"I am here to help in any way you need. Maybe it would be a good idea to get your people involved again with the rebuilding of the village and cleaning up around the island. It is safe for everyone now that we removed the bombs."

"Yes, that is what I plan to do, Branyrd. I need to gather everyone together to ensure them that we will be able to get our island back the way we want it and to give those who lost their lives a proper burial. It is time to do that now so we can move on."

"Now that is how a leader thinks, Kamalnayo. Your people need your leadership and guidance. Benedicto and I will help you do this."

"Thank you both for all you have done. I know I haven't been showing my gratefulness so far. I have spent too much time dwelling on being the leader without demonstrating my leadership in a positive way."

Branyrd smiled with relief and nodded to Kamalnayo as she watched him step out onto the beach and call out to his people to come forward.

"My people and those of Wanalami please come forward. I have a message of utmost importance to relay to you."

Everyone came out of the huts and gathered in front of Kamalnayo with expectant eyes and ears, tuned in to his words.

"First, I want all of you to show your appreciation to our two benefactors, Branyrd and Benedicto. They have made this possible for us to live together in peace and security. If not for them we would be unable to move around the island without a danger of being blown up by the bombs that lay around. Second, I want all of us to get along as brothers and sisters. We need one another in order to complete the tasks that we have ahead of us. There is much to do to rebuild our village and make our island beautiful once again."

There were murmurs of agreement and nodding of heads as the natives looked at one another and bowed their heads at Branyrd and Benedicto, who smiled and nodded back to them.

"I want everyone of you to go back to the village and finish the work you started to rebuild our homes. Once we have this completed, we will have a memorial for all those who lost their lives and give them a proper burial at sea. We will have much to celebrate when we are through. Does anyone have any questions or concerns they want to share with me before we begin our tasks?" Kamalnayo looked over the crowd with a stern expression sure to discourage anyone from speaking.

Branyrd chuckled to herself as she observed the hush that fell over the people as they got up and walked toward the village to begin their cleanup.

She and Benedicto whispered, "Well, it looks like he has control of his people and those of Marnolani. Let's help them move some of the lumber closer to the area so they can begin. We can also look for bodies within the rubble and bring them to the beach. It would be too difficult for others to do that especially if they are one of their own family."

"I agree, Angel. We may not find much left though with all the explosions in the buildings that destroyed everything inside including the people."

"We will do what we can to bring closure for these people so they can begin anew."

Branyrd and Benedicto searched all the destroyed buildings and pulled out bodies that they could find. Other bodies were just scattered pieces that they put in a pile and wrapped in palm leaves and laid beside the bodies on the beach.

Some of the natives watched them and cried as they recognized one of their own. They knelt next to the bodies and prayed, tears coming in floods once again.

Branyrd whispered to Benedicto, "Maybe it wasn't such a good idea to do this now. They can't work if they are like this. They are too distraught."

"Yes, let's pray with them and explain what we are doing."

The Angels knelt next to the mourners and prayed raising their heads and hands toward Heaven. The natives stopped praying and listened to them.

When the Angels were finished praying, they spoke softly to the people, "We will take care of your loved ones and get them ready for burial. You must busy yourselves with the restoration of your village."

The islanders nodded and walked away with heads bowed in grief but they did their best to keep busy as they turned every so often to watch the Angels work.

CHAPTER TWENTY-SIX

A few of the natives, including the two men who came over in the plane from Wanalami, gathered outside the building area and spoke softly. One man was the leader of this group and began to explain, "We cannot let our leader be treated this way. We must help him take over this island. This is our new home and we need to control it. The others can go to the rest of the islands and leave this one to us."

One man spoke up, "How do you expect us to do that? Those two people, Angels or whatever they are, control things. We may have to wait for them to leave."

"No, we don't know when they will leave. We can't wait too long. We may be able to turn some of the others our way if we tell them what we want to do."

"The Candlerians will not listen to us. This has been their island for many years since their ancestors. They will not go along with us or leave for one of the other islands."

"Some of our own people are now listening to their leader. They have forgotten Marnolani. They do not show respect to him. That can't be allowed!" one man exclaimed in defiance.

"Yes, that's right! Did you see the way they listened and did what Kamalnayo asked of them? They are like his puppets."

"What are we going to do to stop this from happening and allow Marnolani control of this island?"

"We must speak with him right away and let him know that we are loyal to him and will do his bidding," their leader explained.

"I don't know about that? Marnolani may already have his own plans with his guards. What if he doesn't want to do anything?"

Another man, hissed, "What if he plans to kill Kamalnayo himself?"

"Shh, you can't say that out loud, someone may hear you!"

Branyrd listened to the whispers in the air as she came closer to the men gathered in a huddle.

She crept closer and stood next to them and said, "What are you conspiring to do, gentlemen?"

"Oh, Branyrd! We didn't hear you there. We were just discussing how we would build our homes here on the island," one man said with a stammer.

"Is that so?" Branyrd asked with a smirk. "I see."

"Well, I guess it is time for us to get back to work. Come on, men. We have work to do," the leader of the rebellion urged.

Branyrd watched as the men moved back to the buildings and got to work or pretended to do that.

She went over to the beach where Benedicto was placing the bodies in a line. "I think we have some more trouble brewing amongst the Wanalamians. I overheard them conspiring to harm Kamalnayo so that their leader can take control of the island."

"Do you think that Marnolani wants to do that?"

"I don't know. Maybe we should speak to him about the conspirators and see what he has to say about it. Maybe they are doing this behind his back and he doesn't even know about them."

"That might be a good idea, Angel. Let's finish up here and go find him. He can't be far. Everyone is now in the village and away from the beach. Even Kamalnayo is over there supervising his people."

"Right, but I haven't seen Marnolani or his two guards since they stormed away from the confrontation with Kamalnayo."

"I haven't either, Angel. He can't be far. Let's try the fields behind the huts."

They searched around the area and found the leader sitting in the grass in deep thought.

"Sorry to disturb you, Marnolani, but we think there is something you should know," Branyrd began.

"That's okay. I was just thinking about what Kamalnayo and I were discussing before he threw me out of the hut."

Branyrd nodded and waited.

"What did you want to tell me?" his curiosity was piqued as he observed the serious expressions on the faces of the Angels.

"We overheard some of your men talking about helping you take control of the island. They may be planning something sinister for Kamalnayo."

"What? Was it my two guards?"

"No, I didn't see them amongst the men. In fact, we haven't seen them since they followed you after you walked away from Kamalnayo," Branyrd explained.

"They may be with the ones who are busy building. I told them not to do anything until I discussed what my plans will be."

Branyrd raised her eyebrows at Marnolani and asked, "What do you plan to do? Are you planning to harm Kamalnayo yourself?"

"Well, no, I told them not to do anything. I don't know what I want to do. My people seemed to have accepted the rule of Kamalnayo as you can see by the way they are following his orders to build."

"Well, not all of your men are so inclined," Branyrd reminded him.

"Yes, as you just told me, Branyrd. I'm sorry that they feel that way. I want my people to get along with the Candlerians especially since we are the cause of all this destruction. I am surprised that they are not rebelling against us for what we did to them and their families and homes."

The leader covered his face with his hands and wept. "I have lost my family too on our island in the lava. I watched them burn with my home. I don't know if I can go on and not keep thinking of that. It was horrible. Many others have lost their loved ones on our island that way. I know I must do something to tell them that we will begin a new life here and live in peace. There has been enough death and destruction. We can't go on this way with more."

"Yes, you are the only one who can do that, Marnolani," Branyrd affirmed.

Branyrd and Benedicto walked away and left Marnolani to muse over what he had just said. They only hoped that he would act on his words and as quickly as possible before something happened to destroy the island and its people again.

CHAPTER TWENTY-SEVEN

Marnolani's two guards were hiding behind the huts and overheard the Angels and their leader discussing a takeover of the island by their fellow islanders.

"Who is in charge of this conspiracy?" one guard asked the other.

"Who do you think it is? He is the one who has always wanted control of the island himself. Tano is nothing but trouble."

"But what if we can control him and have him do our bidding? We can tell him that Marnolani asked us to speak to him about taking the life of Kamalnayo."

"Why would we do that? Marnolani didn't ask us to do that."

"But what if we do that anyway? We can take him out of the picture and control the other men. Tano is strong but not on his own."

"Hmm. Yes, I suspect he would not be strong on his own. But why do you want to kill Kamalnayo? He appears to be a good ruler and benevolent to his people."

"Well, I guess he is but he would not be if we pushed him too far. What if we wanted to do something different on this island? Would he be open to our suggestions?"

"What do you want to do differently on the island?"

"I don't know yet. But I think it would be better to have only one ruler on this island."

"Wait a minute! Are you saying that you want to be the leader?"

"Maybe. Don't you think I would be a good leader?"

"No, I don't! I think you are looking for trouble, Goran."

"Listen to me, Ianal, you will listen and listen good or else."

"Or what, Goran? What are you going to do to me, kill me too?"

"You never know. If you go against me, I may have to do just that. Don't try my patience!"

"Stop right there, Goran! We have a nice place to live. Do you think anyone will accept you if you cause trouble like this?"

"Never mind that now. Let's find Tano and his group and see what they have to say for themselves."

"I don't like this at all, Goran."

Ianal followed behind Goran but reluctantly. He was not happy with how his fellow guard was acting. He had to do something to protect the leaders and the island from disaster.

The two guards went from building to building and finally found Tano and the other men. Goran pulled Tano aside and said, "I hear that you are trying to start a rebellion against Kamalnayo."

"How did you hear that? Who told you?"

"Well, someone overheard you and reported to Marnolani. I don't think he is too happy with you right now. He may be coming here to talk to you. What are you going to do then?"

"I...I...don't know. Are you on our side or are you against us?"

"Hmm, let me think about it for a minute," Goran mused.

"Well, what about it, Goran? Are you for or against us?"

Before Goran could say another word, Marnolani was next to them wearing an expression that would have frightened even Benedicto.

"Well, what are you going to say, Goran?"

Goran gulped down his words, shut his mouth, shook his head and bowed his head.

"I thought so, Goran. You and I have much to discuss. As for the rest of you, I want to know what you were planning to do behind my back."

"Nothing, Marnolani. I...we were not planning to do anything."

"It doesn't sound that way to me. I am waiting for an explanation from one of you now."

The men bowed their heads and mumbled apologies. "Sorry, sir. We... did ...not mean anything by this. It was not us. It was ...Tano who wanted to take over," one man stumbled through the explanation.

"All right. Then you are all excused from this meeting, except Tano, but remember if I hear anything more about this, I will have your heads. Do you understand?"

"Yes...yes, we understand," the men uttered in shock before racing away to work again.

CHAPTER TWENTY-EIGHT

Tano stood in front of Marnolani and bowed his head. He could not look the leader in the eye for fear of being killed on the spot.

The two guards, Goran and Ianal, stood behind their leader but did not say a word. They waited for Marnolani to speak.

"What do you say for yourself, Tano?"

"I…I…made a terrible mistake, Marnolani. Please forgive me. I didn't mean anything by what I said. I would never harm you. You have been a virtuous leader who is also benevolent." Tano kept his head bowed and crossed his fingers behind his back as he prayed that the leader would forgive him by showing kindness in this situation.

"What do you think I should do with you for punishment, Tano?" Marnolani commanded as he lifted the man's chin up to meet his eyes.

"I…I…don't know. Maybe you should make me work harder than anyone else here rebuilding the village."

"Hmm, maybe. Do you think you will do as I say and not go against me again if I do this?"

"Yes, I will do whatever you command me to do, Marnolani. I am truly sorry. I don't know what I was thinking,"

"Okay, I will let you off easy this time. But you must work harder than anyone else. I will be keeping a close watch on you. Now get to work. I expect these buildings will be up to living conditions before the end of this day."

"Yes, Marnolani. Of course, I will get right on it!" Tano backed away with his head bowed until he was far enough away and then raced over to the buildings to work, for his life depended on it.

Marnolani turned to his two guards. "Now, what am I going to do with you two?"

Goran met his eyes with the determined stare of his own defying his leader while Ianal bowed his head in contrition.

"By looking at you both I can see who is the trouble-maker here. Ianal, you are excused. But don't think I won't be watching you closely too."

"Yes, sir. I will go right to work with Tano." The man backed away similarly to Tano as he ran over next to him to work.

"Goran, did I hear you correctly say that you want to be leader here on the island and threaten to take out both myself and Kamalnayo in order to do that?"

"I...I...don't think either one of you is doing a good job."

"Do you think you could do better? Is that what you are proposing?"

"Well, I think I could," Goran kept his voice from faltering but cleared it first before continuing, "Yes, I think I would do things differently."

"Now tell me what you think you would do differently if you were the ruler here."

"First of all, I would ensure that all my people and the people of Candle Island will obey me. They must never question my allegiance to this island and to its people. I would make sure that the island is inhabitable before the next storm comes this way, and fortify it in every possible way to stabilize the buildings."

"I see. You have big plans as a ruler, Goran. Too bad that you will never see them to fruition." Marnolani's eyes were like daggers in Goran's heart as he looked at the ruler.

"Don't you think I would be a good ruler?"

"No, I do not! First, you already betrayed me after all this time you have professed to follow my rules and word as your leader."

"But that was because you were not doing a good job especially since we arrived here. You have done nothing but fight with Kamalnayo and dismiss your guards without giving us any instructions as to what you intend to do here."

"You maybe right there, Goran, but you are not correct in stating that I do not know what I want to do while we live here. Kamalnayo and I had a disagreement but we will come to a consensus soon. What we need are people who listen to instructions and attend to what they need to do and stay out of the business of the rulers."

"You will be detained in my custody under watch by two new guards that I will appoint. You are no longer one of my guards, for you cannot be trusted."

"But…but…I can help you. I just need a chance to prove it."

"Too late for that, Goran. I know that you are no longer trustworthy. Come with me."

Marnolani marched a disgruntled ex-guard to the building site and called over two men who he knew were loyal.

"You two will now be my new guards. You are responsible for keeping Goran detained in my hut. You will tie his hands and feet and keep him there until I give you orders to release him. When it is time for him to be fed you will give him a meal and allow him to relieve himself outside the hut. Then you will retie him and put him back in the hut. Do you understand?"

"Yes, Marnolani. We understand and will do what you ordered." The two men took Goran by his arms and brought him back to the leader's hut where he would stay under their guard.

Goran whispered threats to the two men as they pulled him along. They did not look at him or allow him to intimidate them, for they knew what would happen to them if they did. They were pleased to know that their leader felt them trustworthy of this honor.

Mortan and Miriam watched as the three men passed by their hut. They had overheard the arguing between the men previously and suspected what was happening.

"Do you think that Marnolani will have him killed?" Miriam asked her husband.

"No, I don't think so, for if he wanted that the man would already be dead. Our ruler would have done the same thing, don't you think?"

"Probably. But I think he would have used more force to convince the man to listen to him without violence," Miriam added.

"I don't think this man wants to listen to reason, Miriam. He has one thing in mind and that is to control everyone else. That is a dangerous thing."

"Is that right?"

"Yes, it is, dear. We must mind our own business. It does not concern us," Mortan responded with a sad sigh as he said a silent prayer that nothing bad would happen to either ruler. "We need to do all we can to help the Angels watch over the children. They are innocents in all this."

"I agree, dear," Miriam said as she hugged her husband and kissed his wrinkled cheek. "You really are an Angel yourself. You have never raised your voice to me or uttered a sharp word like other men. I am blessed to have such a kind and caring husband as you."

"There is no need to thank me. I do what I feel is in my heart and that is to love and be loved. There is no room for anything else in my heart, my love."

The woman wiped tears from her eyes as she held on tightly to her husband of more years than she could remember. Time passed and it really didn't matter as long as they could be together for many more years. But she feared that those years would be coming to an end sooner rather than later.

CHAPTER TWENTY-NINE

The Angels were busy stacking more bodies that they continued to find scattered amongst the ashes and debris. The natives watched them with tear-filled eyes as their loved ones were left on the beach to be made ready for their last journey.

"My heart aches for these people who have lost loved ones. There are too many here and some are just small children. How can something like this happen, Benedicto?"

"It is all up to HIM. We cannot judge what is right or wrong. HE has already taken them to live with HIM so they are not suffering any longer."

"No, they are not, but their families who survived are still suffering and will continue to mourn them for their lifetimes."

"Yes, HE knows that and will comfort them as we must do while we are here."

"I'm trying hard to do that but my heart is mourning along with them and breaking in two. How can I not feel this way?"

"You will continue to feel this strongly if you are here. Once we are back in Heaven you will be able to understand better about HIS plans for everyone on Earth."

Branyrd sighed heavily as she lifted one more body and placed it gently next to the others. She looked up and noticed three men walking toward Marnolani's hut.

"What are those men doing with that man. Isn't that one of the ruler's guards?" Branyrd asked in surprise.

"It looks like it. He must be out of favor with the ruler and being detained."

"But what could he have done? I already relayed what I overheard from the other men to Marnolani. Maybe this guard was part of the plot."

"Could be. We will know soon enough, Branyrd. Look who is coming this way."

Marnolani strode with long strides toward the Angels on the beach. He looked like a man on a serious mission.

"Branyrd, Benedicto, may I have a word with you?"

"Of course, Marnolani. What is it? You look troubled," Branyrd stated with concern.

"That is quite right, Branyrd. I am upset with my guards and some of the others, as you know, who are conspiring to overtake leadership of this island from Kamalnayo and me."

"Your own two guards were in on the plot?" Benedicto asked.

"Yes, it seems so but it's a little more complicated. One of my guards, Goran, who is a willful man and has tested my patience in the past, has admitted to wanting to take the role of ruler of the islands of the archipelago from Kamalnayo and me."

"That is not a good sign when you can't trust your own guards," Branyrd said as she exchanged glances with Benedicto.

"What do you plan to do to him, Marnolani?" Benedicto queried.

"For the time being he is under close guard and will stay that way until I can speak with Kamalnayo. I am on my way over to see him now to discuss this. I wanted the two of you to know in case something happened to either one of us. Can you keep an eye on my two guards to ensure they do their job of watching Goran. I don't know who of my people I can trust, but I do know I can trust both of you."

Benedicto nodded and so did Branyrd. "Of course, we will be close by to watch over them. If you need us in any other way, please let us know."

Branyrd whispered, "I was afraid of this, Benedicto. There is always a rebellion when there are too many rulers in an area. The two rulers must come to terms with this and figure a way to make peace amongst their people. If they do not, there will be more deaths."

"Yes, unfortunately that is true, Branyrd. I don't want to see that happen. We will keep an eye on these two and Goran too. He may have something more planned to escape and somehow harm one of the rulers."

Branyrd thought over the problem and concluded. She called out to the guards. "Why don't you two get something to eat. I will watch over Goran."

"We cannot do that. Marnolani will have our heads if we leave here."

"No, he told me to watch over Goran. It's all right for you to take a break."

"Okay," the guards looked at each other and then nodded to the Angel. "We will be back shortly though."

"That's fine. Take your time." Branyrd watched the men walk away and then went into the hut to see Goran.

"Why are you here, Branyrd? Did Marnolani send you?"

"No, Goran. He did not. I came on my own to see you and find out what you plan to do."

"I will not say anything to you. You will share whatever I said with Marnolani and get me into more trouble."

"I don't think you can be in any more trouble than you already are, Goran."

"Maybe not but I don't want to take any chances. Besides, what are you going to do about what I plan?"

"Oh, I don't want to do anything. Your punishment is with Marnolani to decide."

"Do you think you could talk to him for me? He likes you. Maybe you can convince him that I am a good man and really didn't mean what I said."

"Are you? Did you mean what you said?"

"I…umm…I am not going to say anything to you. I need to relieve myself. Can you take me out of here and cut my ties?"

"No, I will get you a basin so you can use it until the men return. They will be right back."

Branyrd turned to leave but was called back by Goran, "What do you think Marnolani will do to me? Will he kill me?"

"I don't know. He did not share that with me. What do you want him to do?"

"I want to live. Maybe I was wrong about wanting to be ruler. It is more difficult than it seems."

"What would you do to one of your men if they defied you as ruler?"

"I…I would probably have them killed by one of my men because I don't think I could trust anyone who did that to me."

"Ahh, I see."

Branyrd left the hut and could hear Goran calling out to her. "Branyrd, where are you? I didn't mean that. I wouldn't kill anyone. Don't tell Marnolani what I said, please!"

Branyrd waited outside the hut listening to Goran's pleas until the two guards returned to take their posts.

CHAPTER THIRTY

Marnolani and Kamalnayo were in deep discussion after what had transpired with Marnolani's men.

"Do you think that this guard of yours can be trusted if we let him live?"

"I have been thinking the same thing, Kamalnayo. I don't know. He is devious and wily, for sure. I have had a difficult time keeping him in line. That is why I gave him the role of guard, so I could keep a close watch over him."

"But it doesn't look like that worked, did it, Marnolani?"

"It does not, but I cannot kill him. I am a benevolent ruler and do not take to violence to rule. I know there is a way to get to him and make him into a better man."

"How do you plan to do that?" Kamalnayo asked.

Before he could answer, there was a knock on the door of the hut.

"Come in," Marnolani called out.

Branyrd stood there and came forward. "Sorry to interrupt you in your discussion but I think Goran may want to say something to you, Marnolani. I think he wants to be forgiven and given a second chance."

"Really? How do you know that, Branyrd?"

"Oh, I suspect that he wants to make restitution for his errant ways."

"Well, I guess I will find out what he has to say for himself. He must have had some time to think things over."

Branyrd smiled and left the hut satisfied that maybe there would be some good would come out of her talk with Goran. She only hoped it helped him come to his senses or else. She could not stand by and watch a man's life taken and would do all she could to convince both men that it was not the thing to do, that there is always another way.

Benedicto smiled at Branyrd and winked giving her his weird eyebrow thing. "Well, what was that all about? Are you up to something, Angel? I can see it in your eyes, they are sparkling with mischief."

"Not me! I am minding my own business and hoping that things will work out for all."

"Hmm, I see." Benedicto poked the Angel in the side as they walked back to the beach.

Branyrd smirked at him and pushed him back with a giggle.

Tano and Ianal worked non-stop, afraid to even glance back to see if Marnolani was keeping a watch over them. They pushed the other men to do the same and soon one building was complete and they moved on to another. The men only stopped to get some water from the children who carted it back and forth with some fruit to help recharge the workers.

Ianal drank his fill and looked at Tano. "Do you think Goran will be killed for his trouble-making?"

"I don't know, but I do know that Marnolani was angrier than I have ever seen him," Tano exclaimed with a shudder. "I'm glad that his wrath was not directed toward me. I was worried that I would be taken out to sea and drowned. That is the easiest way for them to kill us. Our bodies will end up there anyway."

"I guess so, Tano. But I have never known Marnolani to do that to anyone. But of course, I don't know of anyone who would have done what Goran did either."

"Let's get back to work, Ianal. We will hear about Goran's fate soon enough. Our leader will want us to know what happens to those who do not stay loyal to him."

Ianal nodded and shuddered as he snuck a peek over his shoulder to make sure that Marnolani wasn't watching them or listening in to their conversation.

***

Goran was sitting on the floor of the hut and waiting for someone to come get him and mete out his punishment. He was a good swimmer if they tried to drown him but he could not fight off more than two of them to stay afloat. He began to sweat and pray that they would come and get it over with. He kept shaking his head at his stupidity about sharing his thoughts with Branyrd. He should never have done that. What was he thinking? He had to apologize and show that he didn't mean what he said or he would not see another day, for if they did not come get him soon, he was sure to die of imagining what they would do to him.

Branyrd peeked inside the hut and saw Goran with his head down on his knees. When he looked up his face was blanched and he was sweating. She only hoped that he was having second thoughts about doing anything like that again before Marnolani came to see him. She moved away from the window of the hut and hid behind to wait for the ruler.

Marnolani asked Kamalnayo to come along with him but to wait outside until he gave him a signal to come into the hut. His signal would be two taps on the door.

Two rulers were even more intimidating than one, he thought as he opened the door with a flourish to see Goran on the floor looking up at him with a frightened expression.

"Goran, how are you doing? Have you given some thought to what you did wrong?"

"Yes...yes, I did, Marnolani. I am sorry for such outrageous remarks. There is no way that I would be a better ruler than you are. I don't know the first thing about what a ruler is supposed to do or how to punish those who disobey."

"Hmm, so what do you think I should do with you, Goran?" Marnolani met Goran's eyes with his nastiest stare.

Goran shivered and shrunk away from the ruler as he bowed his head. "I don't know. I..."

"What do you suggest I do then? What would you do as ruler?"

"I...I...don't want to be ruler and have to decide someone's fate of life or death.," Goran said in a tremulous voice.

"Hmm, well then, maybe I should get a second opinion on your fate." Marnolani tapped the door twice and waited for Kamalnayo to come in.

CHAPTER THIRTY-ONE

Goran sat up straighter as he looked at the person standing in the doorway. His form filled the whole space there since he was an impressive man of well over six feet tall and broad through the shoulders, not nearly as large as the other man, Benedicto, but closer than any of the other natives.

"Hello, Goran. How do you want to be punished for your crimes?" Kamalnayo asked, hands on hips with a stern expression.

"I...I...do not know. I am sorry. I told Marnolani the same thing. I didn't mean anything by what I said."

"Is that right? Well, then, Marnolani, what should we do with this man? There are a few ways we can punish him on this island. One is to drown him and let his body be eaten by the sharks, another way is to ostracize him to the other side of the island and let him fend for himself, or we can put him in a boat and let him find his way to another island outside of this archipelago."

"Hmm, good suggestions, Kamalnayo." Marnolani winked at the other man, turning his back on Goran.

"But...but...where will I go if you do the third thing. There are no islands close enough now that Wanalami is gone."

"Oh, so you choose the third one, did you, Goran?" Marnolani asked with raised brows.

"No, I didn't choose anything. I was just making an observation."

"What do you think about the first two suggestions, Goran?" Marnolani asked with a smirk.

"I don't like the idea of being eaten by sharks but being ostracized to the other side of the island where it is desolate might not be too bad," he sighed heavily.

"Do you think you could survive on your own there, Goran?"

"I would try to do what I could."

"Wouldn't you be lonely all by yourself? Aren't you afraid of dying alone there?"

"I don't have any friends anyway and no wife or children to mourn my loss."

"Is that so?" Marnolani asked with a sigh.

"I'm sorry to hear that, Goran," Kamalnayo voiced his thoughts too.

"No one likes me anyway. Do what you will with me. I am already dead."

"Well, we will leave you to think about this a little longer, Goran. Maybe you will come up with a suggestion as to what we should do with you."

Both rulers left Goran to his own devices for a little longer and conferred, "Leaving him there to think about the possibilities might be enough of a punishment," Marnolani said to Kamalnayo.

"You may be right, Marnolani. He already appears to be broken and giving up his rebellious ideas. Maybe we should leave him and come back later and see what he has to say for himself."

Marnolani instructed the two new guards to keep watch over Goran, "Stay here and give him water and food and let him relieve himself if he needs to. We will be back later."

"Yes, sir. We will," the two guards said in unison and stood outside the door.

Branyrd had been listening behind the hut and skirted around the area and back to see what was going on with the others who were working on the buildings.

She was quite impressed with how much had been completed from the last time she had been there. The two rulers were standing side by side and instructing the men what to do next.

Benedicto came alongside her and whispered, "Looks like the two men are getting along now and working in tandem with each other."

"Yes, it seems that way for now. It most likely was due to the insurrection by Goran and the others. It made them turn toward one another for support."

"Did you find out anything about Goran's fate? I saw you hiding behind the hut when the two leaders went in to see Goran."

"Yes and no. There has not been a decision made yet. They have given Goran three choices and are letting him stew over them before they go forward."

"What were his choices?" Benedicto asked, already knowing what they were because he was listening too further behind Branyrd but didn't want her to know that.

Branyrd explained and waited for some reaction from Benedicto. "Well, what do you think about that? Will Goran choose to leave the island or be ostracized to the other part?"

"Well, we know that the first choice is out of the question, being eaten by sharks, but the other two are possibilities."

"Do you think that they will not do anything to him after all, but keep a close watch on him?" Branyrd queried.

"That is another possibility. Leaving Goran alone to think this over is like a punishment, don't you think, Angel?"

"Yes, I do. I think Goran is suffering inside there not knowing what to do or what they will do to him. Maybe he needed a wake-up call about his rebellious nature."

"I agree, Benedicto. He needs to know that he cannot do whatever he wants and pull others into his crazy schemes."

While the Angels were discussing the trouble-maker's fate, Goran was trying to get out of his restraints and run away.

He didn't want to wait any longer. He was getting more and more frightened that they would throw him to the sharks and be done with him once and for all.

He kept struggling and then stopped when he heard the door open. He wasn't expecting to see this person here.

CHAPTER THIRTY-TWO

The old man stood over Goran and knelt to look at him. "What did you do, young man?"

"Who are you?"

"I am Mortan. I am the oldest native on Candle Island. I am a generation of many of my kind before me. I am known to be a wise one."

"Well, you sure sound like you think highly of yourself, Mortan. Why are you here?"

"You didn't answer my question, Goran. What did you do to deserve to be locked up here?"

"If you are so wise how come you don't know that, Mortan?" Goran mocked the old man.

"I have an offer for you. Are you going to listen to me or will you continue to mock me and show disrespect for an elderly person?" Mortan's voice became stronger and his eyes took on a lightning-like spark.

Goran sat up straighter and blinked his eyes in surprise as he nodded to the old man.

"Well, I think you need someone to watch over you. I never had a child of my own. My wife and I couldn't have any children but we have taken care of plenty of little ones on the island that have needed our care. I think I can handle someone your age too, if you will listen, learn, and try hard to do what I tell you to do. It is for your own good."

"What can you do for me, Mortan? As you can see, I am not going anywhere. Marnolani is in charge and will not let me go. He may even have me killed for my insubordination."

"I will have a talk with Marnolani and see if I can change his mind. He is a fair man and will not act harshly if the person who has committed an offense shows that he is remorseful. Are you not repentant?"

"Well, I…"

"No, you cannot hesitate. You must feel it in your heart that you are sorry for what you did. Don't you understand, if you don't, he may be forced to do what he does not want to do."

"What can you say to change his mind?"

"I cannot do anything unless you show that you are repentant? You must do this if you want to survive. Do you, Goran?"

"Yes…yes…I am sorry."

"All right then. I will be back after I speak to Marnolani."

Mortan left the man to his own thoughts and took his time finding Marnolani. The longer Goran had to think about things he had told him, the better.

Marnolani was in deep discussion with Kamalnayo at the site of the village. The rulers turned when they heard someone's footsteps behind them.

"What can we do for you, old man?" Marnolani asked.

"I am Mortan and the oldest living native on Candle Island. I have been here since I was born and I am a descendant of the original settlers here. I have something I would like to discuss with you about Goran."

"Hmm, I see. What is that, Mortan?" Marnolani asked with a frown after exchanging confused looks with Kamalnayo.

"I have been to see Goran and he claims that he is remorseful for what he has done. I want to take him under my charge and help him be a better man. I can see there is good in him. It isn't all evil. We all have some of both in us. It is what we do with the good to control and outshine the evil that is important."

"You have much confidence in what you can do with him. I can't say that I have as much assurance in Goran's chances to turn around and do good. What makes you think you can do something with him?"

"I never had any children of my own but my wife and I have taken care of plenty of the children on this island and their parents too. It is easier to do this with someone else's children than your own. I will make him work hard and atone for what he has done. I am a relentless taskmaster. My wife will tell you that," Mortan guffawed.

The two rulers smiled at the man's words. "I will think about this, Mortan. Thank you for coming to see me. Goran needs to spend more time with his thoughts and not be given a reprieve just yet."

"I agree. He does seem as if he is trying to listen better. At first, he was rude to me but once I spoke up to him in a strong voice he caved and listened to what I had to say."

"That is good to hear, Mortan. Maybe you would be good with him. I don't know if he ever had a father to lead him in the right direction. Maybe that is his problem," Marnolani said with a sigh.

"Thank you, Marnolani, for taking the time to listen to me. I will await your word."

"I will come and see you. Are you in the small hut set back off the beach?"

"Yes, that is where you will find me and my wife, Miriam." Mortan backed away and left the rulers to discuss what he had said.

Marnolani turned to Kamalnayo and asked, "What do you think about that old man wanting to take on this imbecile?"

"I think Mortan is a brave and strong man from what I have seen. He has a kindness about him that radiates around and touches everyone who meets him."

"That sounds like something Branyrd would say, Kamalnayo."

"Yes, I guess she would say that. But I feel there is goodness in him and he finds some good in Goran. It might be a sound idea to let him take the man under his wing and bring out the good in him. Mortan could be successful in making Goran into a better man."

"I was thinking along the same lines as you, Kamalnayo. That is the thing to do to get Goran out of our hair. I feel he is troubling no matter what Mortan says. If Goran has someone watching him closely and monitoring his work that would be the best way to go with his punishment."

"Well, maybe you should go see Mortan and tell him so then you can get on with more important matters like helping me rule this island so I can return to my home on the Peeples Islands. I can't stay here forever. My family is waiting for me and so are the rest of my people. You know where you can find me. I trust you to be an honest and kind ruler who will take care of my people and yours and make them feel comfortable. Soon all our people will become one here like a family."

"I will do my best, Kamalnayo. Thank you for your kindness in accepting all of us despite what we did to this island and its people. I must confess that the planes were borrowed from other islands that convinced me that they could help get Candle Island for me. I didn't realize what damage and destruction they would cause. I am truly sorry about all of that. Can you forgive me, Kamalnayo?"

"I am not surprised. I think I know of the islands you speak of. They have been trying to take over my islands for a long time. Don't worry. I will handle them in good time. For now, we have work to do."

"Thank you, Kamalnayo. I hope the people here will forgive me for everything and come to love me as their ruler as they do you. You will always be the ruler, Kamalnayo. I will just be your assistant ruler here. Come back again soon. It will be good to spend time together and compare how things are going."

"Thank you. I will be back, Marnolani. I think we will be friends as well as rulers on these islands. I don't think you will have to worry about my people here. They already accept you and can see you are a benevolent ruler."

"I hope they do because I am not a violent man and never profess to know how to handle all situations especially like Goran's. There never has been anyone to turn against me like that. But I will be keeping close watch over him as Mortan tries to mold him into a better man."

"Mortan has a tough job ahead of him but I think he can do that. Well, I'd better gather my men to get the boat ready for our departure. I will see you again soon. If you need me, send a couple of your men to the next island to get me. Good luck, my friend."

"See you soon, Kamalnayo. Safe travels back home."

The two Angels watched from above, out of sight, as they flew by catching the latest conversation between the leaders. They traveled over to see what was going on at the hut where Goran was being housed. There was a discussion going on between the guards and things didn't look good.

CHAPTER THIRTY-THREE

Marnolani was walking over to the hut of Mortan and his wife when he noticed his two guards arguing about something outside of the hut where he kept Goran a few huts over.

"What is going on over here, men? Is there a problem?"

The two guards came to attention and shook their heads but didn't meet the ruler's eyes.

"Something is wrong. You better tell me quickly."

"Well, we went in to get Goran so he could relieve himself but he wasn't there."

"What do you mean he wasn't there? Where did he go?" Marnolani's voice raised an octave in alarm.

"We don't know. It was time for lunch and we took turns eating and then we were going to get something for Goran after he relieved himself but the hut was empty."

"Wait here. I will be back. Keep a lookout for him."

"Yes, sir!" both men responded in unison with nervous expressions as they looked around for any sign of the perpetrator.

Marnolani calmed down and watched Kamalnayo as he sailed away from the island with a few of his guards. He waved back when he saw Kamalnayo's hands raised to him. Many of the islanders were also there to send him off with a wave and blessing.

Turning back to the hut of the old couple, Marnolani hurried on his way determined to find out what happened to Goran and how he had escaped.

The old couple answered the door and stepped back when they saw the fierce expression of displeasure on Marnolani's face.

"Is everything all right, Marnolani?" Mortan asked in confusion.

"Well, that is what I want to ask you, Mortan. Did you take Goran out of the hut?"

"No, I would not do that without your permission. I have been waiting to hear from you about your decision. I was just explaining what I plan to do with Goran to my wife."

Marnolani nodded at the old woman and continued, "It appears that Goran has escaped. My two guards do not know where he is and never saw him leave."

"Do you know anything about that, Mortan?"

"No, I do not. I told you I would not go behind your back without your consent about what I proposed."

"I see. I believe you, Mortan. Please forgive my impertinence. I can see you are a man of your word. I was coming this way when I noticed that my two guards were in deep discussion about something. I need to find him. As you know, he is not a man who can be trusted despite what you think about the good in him. The evil is taking over and he is up to something."

"I am here to help you find him, Marnolani. Just say the word. I can gather a few more men to help search."

"Yes, that would be a good idea, Mortan. Thank you."

Marnolani sighed and left the hut to begin his own search. He suspected that Goran might be hiding in one of the abandoned huts that were in disrepair and hadn't been touched yet by the workers.

As he looked through one of them, he spotted Branyrd and Benedicto heading his way.

"You look like you may need our help, Marnolani," Branyrd announced as she pulled Benedicto alongside for assistance.

"Yes, I will need all the help I can get. Goran has escaped before I could decide what his punishment would be. Can you assist in checking over the other side of the island while I do this side with Mortan and my men?"

"Of course, we will go there right away and see if he is hiding there. Come on, Benedicto, let's go."

"Let me know as soon as possible if you find him there. Thank you for your help," Marnolani said as he watched them fly away.

***

Earlier Goran had found a sharp piece of wood on the floor and worked it against his bonds until they became loose enough to take off. He had managed to untie his hands and feet and jump out of the back window of the hut when the guards were busy eating.

He didn't trust the old man and Marnolani to forgive him and treat him with kindness. It would not go well in front of the others and make the leader appear weak in their eyes. He had to take things into his own hands even if he had to live on the other side of the island and somehow survive on his own.

He had slipped away through the trees and passed the building site without anyone seeing him. He kept moving as quickly as he could to find a place to hide until dark. He knew that Marnolani would be searching for him soon and his punishment would be swift and merciless.

Goran knew that he could find food in the ocean and in time build a shelter to keep out of the sun and rain and sleep at night. He came across a depression in the earth that would be a safe place to lie down in and cover himself with palm leaves until he could move again.

He worked quickly and dug a larger hole, gathered the palm leaves and laid some on the bottom and more on top of himself as he got comfortable and out of sight.

197

Soon he heard voices coming his way. He curled up into a ball and held on tightly to the palm leaves that were all around him as he waited.

Marnolani's voice was raised as he called out to his men, "Keep searching. He could not have gotten too far. We need to cover every bit of this area while the Angels cover the skies. They may spot him sooner than we can."

Goran shivered as he thought of the Angels looking down and seeing him. What was he going to do if they discovered his hiding place? Where was he going to go then?

The men circled around the hole afraid to step on it and fall in. They didn't see Goran hiding there and moved forward side by side.

Branyrd and Benedicto looked down from above and kept their eyes glued on the area near the beach and between the palm trees. There was no sign of the man.

"Where do you think he could have gone, Benedicto? There are no huts on this side of the beach. Maybe he is hiding amongst the trees where they are thickest along with the other low bushes and high grasses. This part of the island has been untouched. No one comes here by the looks of it."

"I agree, Angel. But this is the only place he can go to escape. He is smart and will find a place to hide out until dark and then move toward the trees where he can build a place to stay. He will have to move sooner than later just to find food and water too."

Goran listened to the Angels talking and closed his eyes and hugged himself for it was getting cooler sitting in the hole with only his sandals and shorts and top. The earth felt damp and he could feel a sneeze coming on. He covered his mouth and nose to muffle the noise. He only hoped that the Angels didn't have exceptional hearing.

CHAPTER THIRTY-FOUR

Mortan and the other men covered plenty of the area around the beach and then moved into the grasses, trees and bushes of the island as they got thicker. They listened for any sounds as they spread out to cover as much area as they could before it got dark. They knew it would be difficult to find their way back then through this dense forest.

Marnolani was moving his men to another area trying to cover the whole island if possible. It was not a large island but large enough to make it almost impossible to search it all in one day on foot. It was not like they had any form of transportation to get around easier. Any animals such as donkeys and goats that they may have had were killed in the bombing.

Back on the beach the children played in the sand and chased Misty around until they were too tired to stand. They headed back to their huts when they heard the voices of the sisters, and others calling them in to eat.

"What do you think is going on? Why is everyone looking around? Who is missing?" Seth asked his sister and new brother.

"I think it must have something to do with the man they took away. He must have done something bad. I saw the two guards take him into the hut over there," Freya announced.

"How do you know that, Freya?" Dack asked with wide eyes.

"Oh, I just guessed because there is no one else they would be looking for that hard."

"Yeah, I guess so," Seth agreed and added, "None of us are lost."

'Right! We are too smart to get lost on our island!" Freya stated with pride.

"Maybe we should go help find the person who is lost and bring him back here," Seth announced.

"Well, we could do that but not before we eat lunch!" Dack said with a grin. "I'm too hungry to go right now."

"Good idea, Dack. Let's go eat first then we will make a plan to find the missing person. They might consider us heroes," Seth stated with a giggle.

"Don't go anywhere unless you tell Mom and Dad first, Seth, or you will be in trouble," Freya instructed him with a frown of impatience.

"I promise, Freya. Don't worry," Seth said as he winked at Dack and went inside to eat.

The two boys ate as quickly as they could and excused themselves after cleaning up their plates as instructed by their mother. They left Misty there who didn't look at all happy to be left behind.

They nodded to one another and went outside to whisper about a plan to find the missing person.

"Dack, I know of a place where this man might go to hide. We need to leave right now so we can be back before it gets dark. Otherwise, we may have to stay there and camp out."

"Camp out? Where would we camp out?" Dack asked in a nervous twitter.

"There's nothing to be afraid of, Dack. I am your big brother and I will protect you from any animals or monsters there."

"There are animals and monsters where we are going? What kind of animals?"

"Well, let's see. There are all kinds of birds, lizards and maybe a donkey, goat or chicken wandering around."

"I'm not afraid of those animals. What about monsters?"

"Hmm," Seth thought and then smiled, "I'm not sure about what kind we may meet. I've never seen any myself. But we must be prepared just in case there are some there."

Dack's eyes got wide and took on a frightened look as he kept glancing around him as they continued to walk further away from their settlement.

Branyrd and Benedicto were listening to the boys and chuckled at their discussion about monsters.

"They really are sweet little boys, aren't they, Benedicto?"

"Yeah, if you call that sweet teasing your little brother who is already frightened," Benedict replied with an arched brow.

"Oh, they are just being boys. Seth doesn't mean any harm to Dack. He loves his new brother and just wants him to look up to him and need him."

"That's a possibility, Angel. I guess I didn't think of that."

"Maybe we better follow them and make sure they are safe from 'monsters' or someone like Goran who could take them for hostages."

"Why would he do that?"

"You never know with a man like Goran. He may feel threatened and use them to keep himself from being harmed."

"Wouldn't you think that his punishment by Marnolani would be worse if he did something so heinous as that?" Branyrd asked as she kept her eyes on the boys as they walked through the trees.

"Yes, I would think so, Angel, most definitely it would be worse. I will go back to the boys' hut and let their parents know where they are, in case they are looking for them. I don't want them to worry," Benedicto said and flew away.

"Good idea, Benedicto. I will follow the boys in the meantime."

The boys finally stopped at a large hole that was covered with palms and branches. They pushed the branches around with their feet and then disappeared.

CHAPTER THIRTY-FIVE

Branyrd strained to see where the boys had gone. One minute they were walking along and the next they had disappeared. She flew down for a closer look.

"Seth, Dack, where are you?" the Angel called out.

"Branyrd, we're down here! We fell into a hole!" Seth's voice sounded strained as though he might be injured.

"Are you all right? Did you hurt any part of your body?"

"I think I hurt my ankle," Seth cried out in pain. "Ow, it hurts!"

"Okay, I'm coming down to help you. Where is Dack? Is he hurt too?"

"I don't know. He is sleeping right now. I tried to wake him up but he didn't move."

"All right. Don't move him or yourself. I am coming down there."

Branyrd pulled aside all the palm leaves and branches and looked down into the hole. The boys were laying on their sides and Seth had his arm around Dack protectively but the boy was not moving.

The Angel reached down and picked up Seth and laid him on the ground outside the hole and then went back down to get Dack. As she put Dack down next to his brother the boy stirred.

"How are you feeling, Dack?" Branyrd asked.

"I…I…think I hurt my head. I have a lump and some blood," he said as he touched his head and looked at his bloody hand.

"Let me see, Dack," Branyrd asked as she tenderly touched the spot that was cut and ran her hand over it saying a prayer.

"It feels better now, Branyrd. Thank you." Dack smiled at the Angel and looked around for his brother.

"Seth is right here, Dack. He was worried about you but took care of you until I could get here."

"Thank you, Seth. It's good having a brother." Dack's eyes filled as he gave Seth a hug.

"It's okay. That is what brothers do, Dack. I am your big brother and I am supposed to take care of you." Seth's eyes were brimming as he said this but quickly wiped them away before Dack could see.

Branyrd gently touched Seth's ankle when she heard him grunt in pain. "Let me see that, Seth. You have sprained your ankle. Hold still until I can make it better."

"How did you do that, Branyrd? It feels better already."

"HE did that for you and Dack. HE didn't want you to suffer because HE loves you."

"HE does?" Seth and Dack said with a smile. "Well, we love HIM too, don't we Dack?"

"Yup, I do. I feel better and that's a good thing!" Dack wore a wide smile and got up and touched his head again. This time his hand came away clean.

"Where were you two going?"

"We were going to be heroes!" Dack exclaimed.

"Heroes?"

"Yeah, if we found the person who is missing, we would be heroes."

"Well, I guess we could have been heroes, Dack. But we didn't get too far and didn't find the man."

"I think we should get you both home so your parents won't be worried about you. Leave the searching to the adults. Okay?"

"Okay, I guess we have to go home now. But we can tell everyone how we fell into a hole and Branyrd got us out. That probably makes Branyrd the hero."

Branyrd laughed and helped the boys up from the ground.

"Okay, I don't think we can walk," Seth said as he limped around giving Branyrd a sad face.

"How about a ride home?" Branyrd asked with a glint in her eye.

"Hurrah! Let's go!" the boys exclaimed in unison thrilled to have an excuse to fly again.

Back at the huts Benedicto was outside talking to some of the islanders gathered there. The boys' parents were waiting and once they spotted Branyrd flying over with the boys in tow, they ran forward to greet them with Misty barking loudly, happy to see the boys. Freya looked upset and rushed over to see her brothers to scold them and then give them huge hugs in relief.

The boys took their sister's hugs and then bent down to pet Misty who licked their faces all over in joy.

"Where did you go?" their father asked with a stern look.

"We went searching for the missing person," Seth declared.

"Let's get them inside first. Look at them. They are covered in dirt," their mother exclaimed in alarm. "Are you hurt?"

"No, Branyrd fixed us or maybe HE did. She said HE loves us. Right, Branyrd?" Seth announced.

Their parents nodded in thanks to Branyrd and patted their chests to show their relief.

"That's right, Seth. HE loves you all," Branyrd smiled at the parents as she responded to Seth.

"What about the man who is missing? Does HE love him too? He is not a nice man, right?"

"Well, HE loves everyone, good or bad."

"Really?" Dack queried.

"Yes, even the bad ones. But he is disappointed with those who do unkind things."

"Wow!" Seth exclaimed as he exchanged surprised expressions with Dack.

"That does not mean that you can misbehave," their mother said with a frown.

"Okay. We promise we will be good," Seth sighed.

Branyrd winked at the boys and watched them go inside with their parents who hovered over them along with their dog and sister who adored them.

The islanders were returning from their search with Marnolani at the head of the group. Behind them was a bedraggled Goran who was looking anything but happy.

"Where did you find him?" some of the others asked as they got closer.

"He was hiding in the trees underneath a makeshift hut. We heard him sneeze. That gave him away," one man answered with a snicker.

Laughter was heard all around as this message was passed amongst them making Goran look even more upset with himself as he sneezed repeatedly now.

"Sounds like someone is coming down with a cold, huh, Goran?" Marnolani asked as he stifled a chortle.

"Hmm, I'm fine," Goran announced as he sneezed again and again.

"What should I do with you, Goran?" Marnolani asked as he met the man's eyes.

"I didn't do anything wrong. I needed to relieve myself and the guards didn't come for a long time. I couldn't wait any longer."

"Is that right?" the leader retorted with a humph.

The two guards who were holding Goran shook their heads at the leader and held onto Goran's arms tighter to make a point.

"Okay, I really didn't have to go, well, I did but I could hold it a little longer. I didn't want to stay there because...I..."

"Because what, Goran? Were you fearful of your punishment?"

"Well, I...well, yes. I was. I want to make amends but don't know how," Goran cried in exasperation.

"I was coming over to tell you what I had decided when I discovered you were gone," Marnolani stated as he looked at the distressed man.

CHAPTER THIRTY-SIX

Goran waited for Marnolani to continue. He looked back and forth at the others who stood quietly around him with curious expressions as they too waited to hear what their leader would say.

"Well, I spoke with Mortan and he told me that he wanted to take you on as an apprentice. He has plans for you to work with him."

"He already spoke with me but he did not say what he wanted me to do."

"Why don't we go visit Mortan and let him tell you what he has planned for you, Goran."

Marnolani released his guards to step aside so he could take Goran to Mortan's hut. "I won't be needing your help, men.

Report back to the building site and help the others complete the rebuilding. The rest of you can go back to work too."

The two guards nodded and went on their way followed by many others who had stopped to see what was going on.

Mortan was waiting inside his hut with his wife and looked up to see Goran enter with Marnolani.

"I hope we are not disturbing you, Mortan." Marnolani said as he entered, pushing Goran forward.

"Not at all, leader. I see you found our man. He isn't looking too good though. I think he caught something."

"Yes, I think he did," both men chuckled as they observed Goran rubbing his nose and sneezing again.

"He evidently doesn't know about the bushes he was hiding under. They are quite irritating to the nose and can cause sniffles and sneezing for days on end," Mortan stated.

"Really?" Goran asked in alarm.

"Don't worry, it won't last forever. At least you didn't get the rash that goes along with it."

"Rash?" Goran gulped as he checked his body for signs of it.

"Well, don't bother looking. It doesn't always come out the first day. It may surface in a day or so with large welts that weep and drain."

"What?" the distressed man said in exasperation.

Mortan and Marnolani exchanged amused glances as they both tried to keep from guffawing aloud.

Branyrd and Benedicto were close to the back of the hut and chuckled at the exchange.

"Do you think that this is their way of punishing him by tormenting him with illness?" Branyrd asked.

"Maybe. It seems to be working on Goran. Look at him. He can't stop checking his arms and legs for welts," Benedicto snickered.

"It may be time for us to move along. Everything is settling down now," Branyrd said as she frowned.

"Could be soon, Angel. Why the sad face?"

"You know me. I don't like this part of my mission when it's time to leave."

"I know. But just think how much you did for these islanders and how well they have progressed since this all began. You have another successful mission under your belt."

"I realize that, Benedicto. But I hate to leave these people. Maybe there is something else we need to do first."

"HE hasn't told me that this mission is over. We will wait until HE decides it is. Don't frown, Angel. It ruins your lovely face."

"Oh, Benedicto, please don't say silly things to me. I don't care about my face. It is only temporary anyway."

"Well, HE did pick that face for you. I kind of like it myself. It is close to the one you have in Heaven after all, only smaller."

"Hmm. I wonder what I can do to help them more?" Branyrd mused. She would do anything to prolong the time here. She would miss everyone and didn't want to think of having another mission under her belt, so to speak. It was too sad to think about.

Benedicto watched Branyrd as she worked at what she would do next. He smiled and stepped away. She needed time to get herself prepared for the inevitable.

The sisters came forward when they saw Branyrd sitting on the beach by herself.

"Are you okay, Branyrd?" Sister Superior asked.

"Yes, I'm fine, Sister. I was just thinking about everything that has happened so far."

"It has been quite a terrifying time for many. We are thankful for your intercessions, Branyrd, and wanted to come thank you again. We know that you won't be here forever and hate to see you go."

"This is what HE wanted me to do. You don't have to thank me. You should thank HIM."

"Of course, we do that every day in our prayers. I need to ask you something. Will you help us build our orphanage and hospital again? It looks like all the buildings are going to homes or businesses."

"Oh, yes, of course. That is what I need to do. My mission here is not finished. We have to build the orphanage and hospital to take care of the children and sick ones."

The sisters smiled as they watched the Angel's face light up.

Branyrd's smile widened and she sighed happily. "I knew I had more to do. How could I have forgotten about the children. They were my priority."

"Not to worry, Branyrd," Sister Superior said softly. "We have prayed for this to come to fruition. It must be in HIS plans for you to do this."

"Yes, I'm sure it is in HIS plans. Now, where is Benedicto when I need him?" the Angel sighed.

CHAPTER THIRTY-SEVEN

Branyrd hurried over to the building site to pick out a place for the orphanage and hospital. Also, she would build a school for the children. After all, they needed to have a place to go every day to learn about their island, language, and customs.

The Sisters of Love followed closely behind her and suggested different places that would be perfect for all three buildings.

Benedicto appeared behind one of the new buildings and stepped out to greet them.

"Where have you been, Benedicto? I was looking all over for you" Branyrd sighed with a roll of her eyes.

"I was right here all the time keeping track of what was going on. What are you in such a fuss about, Angel?"

Branyrd explained, "We forgot all about building the orphanage, hospital and a school. What were we thinking? The children need a place to go every day to learn about everything around them."

"It's also good to keep them busy and out of trouble," one sister added with a laugh.

"I agree, Sister. Thank you." Branyrd nodded with a chuckle.

Benedicto announced in his loud and powerful voice, "Attention everyone, we have more buildings to do. We need to clear a space for an orphanage, hospital, and a school."

Everyone observed the huge Angel and nodded in agreement. "Yes, let's get to work."

Marnolani was nearby supervising some of the men in clearing out the areas of the endless debris. He came over to the Angels and listened to what they were discussing.

"Yes, I agree with you. We do need these three buildings right away. I will get the islanders busy gathering more wood and palm leaves and whatever else we can find to begin."

Mortan was heading over to the group with Goran beside him. He spoke up, "I have an able-bodied man right here who needs to help. He can do whatever jobs you have."

Goran groaned and hung his head but nodded when asked by Mortan, "Aren't you capable, Goran?"

"Yes...I guess I am."

"Let's go over to the area they just cleared. I will show you what I do when I must use whatever we have to reconstruct something. I have a few tricks up my sleeve, Goran, that I want to teach you."

Goran followed Mortan with his shoulders slumped and dragging his feet. A sneeze would overtake him from time to time and he rubbed his nose to try to stop them.

Branyrd watched the islanders working together peacefully and even Goran appeared to finally be content in working alongside Mortan.

She was in awe of Mortan who gave advice in a kindly way and never raised his voice. He was patient and understanding and took his time explaining what he wanted Goran to do.

If there ever was an Angel here on this island, Mortan was one. She sighed and said a silent prayer. "I hope YOU are not planning on taking Mortan just yet, LORD. He is a true kind spirit who is needed here to guide these people."

"No worries, Angel. He is needed here but I am watching him always. He is a special one."

Branyrd sighed in relief as she turned to go find Benedicto once again. She couldn't bear to see Mortan taken from his people. She had seen others taken before on her previous missions and it nearly broke her heart then.

Benedicto was lifting some of the heavy logs for the men when Branyrd came up behind him.

"There you are. I was looking for you as usual, Benedicto. HE spoke to me about Mortan. HE said Mortan is a special one and HE will be watching over him."

"Did you doubt that HE would do this, Branyrd?"

"Well, no, not really, but I did think HE might take him from here like he did the others on my other missions. I couldn't stand to see him leave his people. Everyone loves him. There is no one better to guide his people along with Marnolani."

"I agree, Angel. I also think that Marnolani knows Mortan's value to him as a man he can trust to help him with the islanders."

The building went on throughout the afternoon and into the evening when everyone stopped to eat and refresh themselves so that they could finish up what they could before it got too dark.

Branyrd and Benedicto stayed behind to work after everyone else had gone back to their huts for dinner and sleep. They planned to do the rest of the building while the others slept. It was the only way to get things completed quickly without them seeing the Angels in action.

They knew that they would have to erase everyone's memories about all the magic that they did such as the flying, bomb clearing and now the building. It would be better for them not to remember all these things, but as before, the LORD would allow the people to remember that there were two kind people who did help them get their lives back together on the island.

Benedicto worked on the hospital building while Branyrd took care of putting up the school and orphanage. She would keep them together so that the children would learn to get along with each other that way.

With the LORD's help maybe all the orphaned children would be adopted by families so that they would not have to go back to the orphanage. If that was the case then the school and orphanage would become one building.

Branyrd looked up and prayed for such a miracle before she had to leave.

In the meantime, Branyrd wanted to make everything as special as she could for the children who were her main mission. She worked with the LORD's help to design a special place just for them. She couldn't wait to see their joy when they discovered what this was.

After this was completed, the Angels lifted the bodies that were on the beach and flew them to the burning island for cremation. There were too many to drop into the ocean. Doing this while the islanders slept was the best way to put the deceased to rest away from the eyes of their loved ones.

CHAPTER THIRTY-EIGHT

Next morning the sun was shining, the air was warm, quite balmy in fact, and the wind was blowing the sand around as all the children ran out to play. They stopped in their tracks when they saw all the buildings in the distance that were now there.

Seth, Dack and Freya called out to the other children," Look at all the buildings over there! Let's check them out!"

When they got closer, Seth shouted out, "Look at the playground! It has swings, slides, and all kinds of things for us to play on. I can't wait to try them all out!"

Word spread quickly and other children came out when they heard the whoops and hollers echoing through the air.

Before long the adults were out of their huts to see what all the noise was about and from which direction it was coming.

The sisters followed the sounds of the laughter of the children and stopped in shock when they saw all the playground equipment that had materialized overnight.

Sister Superior whispered to the other sisters, "We know where all that came from, don't we?" she said as she pointed Heavenward with a smile. They nodded and wiped tears of joy from their eyes.

Others followed behind the sisters, and stopped to admire in wonder how and where it all came from.

Branyrd and Benedicto hid behind the buildings and smiled in pleasure at the joy in the faces of the children. Branyrd's heart filled to overflowing with joy and her eyes with tears.

Benedicto poked her in the arm and offered his sleeve to her to wipe her tears. She shook her head and let the tears rain down for the pure freedom of erasing her emotions that way.

Marnolani was in deep discussion with Mortan about Goran's progress when he saw the people standing around near the buildings. He walked closer and saw what they were looking at. His eyes opened wider and so did his mouth when he saw that all the buildings were now finished and there was a magnificent playground for the children which they were putting to good use and thoroughly enjoying.

Mortan smiled and patted his heart which was fluttering with happiness at the sight of all the children having so much fun.

"Well, it looks like the Angels have been busy all night, Marnolani," Mortan said with a happy sigh.

"Yes, indeed. They have outdone themselves by the looks of it all. They finished the school, orphanage, and hospital.

Though the school looks like it is two buildings in one. Look how they are connected as one."

"Yes, I think Branyrd wanted to make it that way so that the children would be together all day long and not be separated by a building. That way they would not feel different."

"I can see that, Mortan. That was a wonderful idea."

"What else would you expect from an Angel?" Mortan chortled. He looked up and winked at Branyrd and Benedicto who were coming their way.

"You did a splendid job on the buildings, Angels, especially the playground. The children are thrilled! You couldn't have done any more to make them happier," Marnolani stated as he shook the hands of the Angels and patted his chest in thanks.

"Thank you, Angels, for being so generous to the children. As long as they are happy, so am I," Mortan stated with a broad smile.

"It was our pleasure, Marnolani and Mortan. Good to see you both up and about and looking rested. You may need to build some beds and desks for the school and orphanage so that the sisters will have a place to stay each night after they have finished teaching the children."

"Yes, good idea, Branyrd. I'm sure Mortan and the others will finish those up soon. Well, maybe now you both should take some time off and rest after you worked all night to create this beautiful village. The people are also thrilled. Look at them! They are going in and out of each building and shedding tears of joy," Marnolani exclaimed.

Mortan nodded at Branyrd and smiled.

"Their tears are evidence that they love everything we did. That is all the thanks we need. We would do it no matter what for the children to be happy. This was my mission, after all, to take care of the children. Now that I did that, it may be time for me to leave and Benedicto too," Branyrd said with a heavy sigh and a sad face.

"We cannot leave until we see that every child is satisfied with what we have done. Let's go over and ask them if there is anything else they need," Benedicto said as he headed over to the busy playground.

Branyrd followed closely behind after excusing herself to Marnolani and Mortan.

"What could they possibly need now, Benedicto? You know I would do anything for them."

"Of course, Angel. But I think you need to talk to them so that you can have closure. It is not going to be easy to leave here."

"I know...I...know!" Branyrd sniffled and wiped her eyes so that the children would not think she was unhappy.

Dack slid down the slide and jumped off as Branyrd walked by. He yelled out to her, "Branyrd, did you see me slide down? It was so cool! Do you want to see me do it again?"

"Yes, please do it again, Dack!" the Angel yelled back at him.

"Wow, that was perfect, Dack! You really are a good slider!" she followed along with him as he raced to another slide and did it again.

Seth called out to her to get her attention too, "Branyrd, watch me climb the bars! I am like a monkey!"

"Yes, you are, Seth! Good for you!"

Freya and some of the other children came over to see her and ask, "Do you know who did this playground for us?"

Before she could answer, Benedicto said, "Well, I think I know who did this. You are looking at her." He pointed to Branyrd as the kids jumped up and down and then hugged and surrounded her while telling the other children that Branyrd was the one who made all this happen. All the children wore smiles of joy and thanked her again and again as they all took turns giving her another hug before going back to play.

Branyrd sat down on the ground and held her head in her hands as tears kept flowing through them to wet the ground.

"Are you okay, Angel?" Benedicto asked as he bent down to gaze at her in concern.

"I...I...am fine, Benedicto. I feel so much love from the children that it is almost overwhelming how good they are and now I see why the LORD wanted me to save them all. They are so precious and what is good here on Earth."

"Do you still think you need to do more here?"

"Yes, I do. I want to see all the children adopted by the other families. No child should be without parents or guardians to help them grow up."

"I agree, Angel. But what do you plan to do?"

"I will speak to Marnolani and Mortan. They will be able to gather the people and make plans to give the children homes. The sisters will be the teachers in the school so that they will have plenty to do. Some of them may staff the hospital too for that is what they were doing anyway before."

"Well, then we better get moving and put this plan of yours into action, Branyrd. Time is getting short. HE just told me that HE expects us to finish up soon and let the people carry on for themselves. They are ready to do that."

"Okay, but can I just sit here and watch them for a little longer, Benedicto?"

"Do whatever you need to do, Angel. I am right here with you and will be by your side until you are ready to leave."

"Thank you, Benedicto. You are a special kind of Guardian Angel even if you do exasperate me at times." Branyrd smiled but her lips slipped downward as she trembled.

CHAPTER THIRTY-NINE

The children played for a few more hours and then drifted back to their huts in happy exhaustion, ready to eat and rest.

Branyrd watched them leave the playground and sighed. Now it was time for her to move and bring the next part of her plan to fruition.

She poked Benedicto and said, "It is time to speak with Marnolani and Mortan and let them take the reins to put this plan into action. Once that is done, I will be ready, though sadly, to leave."

"Okay, let's go find them. They are probably eating their lunch now but we can wait until they are finished to discuss this plan of yours."

"Right, I can wait a little longer," Branyrd smiled wanly.

"I know this will be difficult for you, Angel. Don't worry; it will work out. Remember you will be given a new mission soon enough. Once you get into another project things will keep you so busy that you won't be feeling gloomy."

"I hope so, Benedicto. I do not like to feel this miserable each time I must leave Earth."

"Let's go wait outside Marnolani's hut for a little while. He will come out when he is finished eating, I'm sure. If he doesn't, we can always knock and ask to speak with him."

"I'll go see if Mortan can meet with you and Marnolani. Maybe he is finished already."

Mortan stepped out of his hut as Benedicto was heading that way and the old man waited for the huge Angel to come to him.

"Were you looking for me, Benedicto?"

"Yes, I was. Branyrd has a plan to help all the children and she wants to present it to you and Marnolani. Are you free to meet now?"

"Of course. Is Marnolani around? I haven't seen him since I went to have lunch with my wife."

"Branyrd is going to find him now."

"What is Branyrd planning? Can you share a little about it with me or do I have to wait for Marnolani?"

"Well, I think Branyrd should be the one to speak with both of you. It is her plan and part of her mission."

"I see. I am a patient man and can wait a little longer. I was just curious to hear what she plans to do about our children. I thought you and she did all you could by saving them and bringing them here to us. We can never repay what you have done to save us all, our island and Marnolani's people."

Before Benedicto could respond to Mortan's words, Marnolani and Branyrd were coming toward them.

Mortan smiled at Branyrd and stepped forward to stand next to Marnolani. Both men kept their eyes on Branyrd waiting patiently for her to explain this unexpected meeting.

Branyrd smiled back at them and began, "My time here is coming to a close, sad to say," she cleared her throat and dabbed at her eyes which continued to seep against her will. "I have done what was expected of me while I have been here but it is not enough. I want each child to have a home with a family and that cannot be unless each orphaned child is adopted by the rest of you."

"Hmm, I see what you mean, Branyrd," Marnolani said with a twinkle in his eyes. "That is quite commendable of you to want to see each child in a happy setting. I agree with your proposal."

Mortan nodded and held his hands over his heart as he responded, "I agree with Marnolani. It is kind of you to think of our children. Turning to his leader he asked, "How do you propose to present this plan to your people?"

"I have an idea that will make everyone happy. Come with me. Gather everyone outside now. We will present this proposition to them about adopting one or more children each."

"Some of us do not have any children of our own and would welcome having one in our lives. I know Miriam and I would be happy to adopt a child. We already adopted a grandchild. One more will only fill our home with more joy." Mortan smiled with tears in his eyes. "I hope we are not too old to qualify."

"No, I don't think you are too old, Mortan. You are a good man and your wife is kind and generous too. You will make wonderful parents." Marnolani patted Mortan on the back to reassure him.

"Thank you, Marnolani. How will we decide which child will become part of our families?"

"Well, let's call everyone out and see how they want to do this."

Branyrd and Benedicto followed them over to the beach in front of all the huts where many were gathering to collect their belongings to move into their new homes in the village a short distance away.

When Marnolani stopped in front of them, the islanders looked up to see what he wanted to say.

"Listen everyone. I know some of you are not too sure of my leadership yet since Kamalnayo returned to the Peeples Island mainland. I will do all I can to take care of all of you and ensure your lives will return to normal and be prosperous."

The islanders nodded and cheered but stopped when he raised his hands to them.

"All of you know Branyrd and Benedicto who have been sent here to aid us in getting our lives back together after all this strife. Branyrd has a proposal that she has presented to me about our children who are orphaned here."

Marnolani turned to Branyrd and called her forward.

Branyrd looked over all the faces of the islanders who were whispering and wearing confused expressions as they turned their attention to her.

CHAPTER FORTY

"I will be leaving here soon and wanted to make sure that I did all I could to help the children to be happy with families of their own. There are so many that are newly orphaned by these tragic events, besides those who were already orphans. I would like to see all children in homes with families of their own. Can you find it in your hearts to adopt a child or children to give them the love and care that they all need and deserve?"

Everyone looked at Branyrd and started talking at the same time. Marnolani raised his hands and spoke, "If you are happy with this suggestion, please raise your hands."

Several hands were raised and then every hand was raised even the children raised theirs in agreement.

Branyrd giggled and clapped her hands when she saw the children's smiling faces and raised hands.

Dack spoke up as he had his hand raised too, "I am already adopted!" he exclaimed in joy as he hugged his new brother, sister, and parents who all wore smiles too. Even Misty barked in agreement.

"Well, then that settles it, doesn't it?" Marnolani exclaimed. "Each family who would like to adopt a child or children step forward. Children step forward and choose your family."

Children ran over to the couples and some single men and woman and gripped their hands.

All children were chosen except one little girl who was hiding behind a tree.

Branyrd went over to talk to her. "What is your name? Why are you hiding?"

"My name is Payla. I don't think anyone will want me. I am not pretty like the others. Look at me! I have a funny nose and lips and I..." the child cried and fell into Branyrd's arms.

"You are beautiful like every child here. Any family would want you as their daughter, Payla."

"Do you think so?" Payla stopped crying when she saw a couple standing behind Branyrd beckoning her forward.

"Come with us, Payla. We don't have any children and would love to make you part of our family."

Mortan and Miriam took Payla by the hands and guided her back to their new home. Payla hugged them as she walked away proudly with her new mother and father.

Benedicto stood waiting for Branyrd to come to him. He could see she was having a difficult time keeping all her emotions in check.

"It's going to be okay, Angel. Look what you have done to make this island a home again for all these people. You have helped them clean all the debris, build homes, and find families for all the orphans. You have done more than was expected of you."

"I...I...wanted to leave here with a good feeling that everyone is going to be happy and live good lives. I think that will keep me from falling apart when I leave."

"Don't worry, Branyrd. HE will make sure that you see how they are all doing after you leave as he did before on the other missions. HE knows how difficult it is for you to leave Earth and all your friends."

"I hope so, Benedicto. I look forward to seeing how they are doing after we leave. Do you think HE will give me a little more time until then?"

"Yes, I think HE will. HE hasn't summoned me, yet."

The islanders and their new children hurried to gather their belongings to continue to move to their newly built village. There was so much excitement in the air as they rushed around with Marnolani's guidance.

Mortan and Miriam held their child, Payla, in their arms as she couldn't stop hugging and kissing them.

Branyrd waved her hands over the girl's disfigured face and smoothed out her lips and nose. Payla touched her face when she felt her nose and lips tingle.

She looked over at Branyrd and smiled. "Thank you, Branyrd. You did something to my nose and lips. They feel better. Now I am beautiful!"

Mortan and Miriam hugged Payla and said, "You were already beautiful, daughter, in our eyes and always will be.'

Palya's eyes filled as she hugged them tight and smiled at Branyrd who waved at her and threw a kiss.

Amara, who was Mortan and Miriam's adopted granddaughter, came forward to introduce herself to Payla, "Hi Payla. I am Amara and we are like sisters now. Your parents are my adopted Mimi and Papa."

"Really? I like having a sister, Amara. Do you want to go to the playground?"

"Can we go play now, Mommy and Daddy and Mimi and Papa?"

"Of course. Don't go too far and be home before it gets dark," Amara's mother said in a voice choked with emotion.

"Have fun little ones," Mortan and Miriam said in unison.

"Okay!" the girls announced in excitement as they held hands and skipped away to the playground.

***

Later that night after everyone was settled in their new homes and had dinner, they gathered around outside the playground, spoke about their ordeal, how they had all survived and how thankful they were.

They called Branyrd and Benedicto over. "Come sit with us. We don't want you to leave. Can you stay a little longer? We need you."

Branyrd sniffled and calmed herself to speak. "We must leave soon but I will check in with you from Heaven to make sure you are all right. HE will allow me to see you one last time."

"But can you come back and visit us again?" Mortan asked.

"No, I'm sorry it is not allowed. Once I complete my mission here on Earth, I must go on to the next one."

The children gathered at Branyrd's feet and hugged her legs. She looked down at them and tried to keep her tears at bay. "I will always miss every one of you. Please be happy with your families and be good, work hard in school for the sisters and remember me as I will always remember you."

Each child waited for Branyrd to bend down to receive a hug and kiss before they returned to their families.

Seth, Freya and Dack were last in line and hugged the Angel tight before letting her go. "We will always remember you, Branyrd and you too, Benedicto. We love you both," Seth stated with tears in his eyes.

"I wish you wouldn't leave us," Dack announced as he cried openly now.

"I will always be with you all here." Branyrd pointed to her heart.

"Oh, is that like you told me before that HE is always there too?" Seth gushed in surprise.

"Yes, that is exactly right, Seth."

"I'm sure I have more than enough room here for you, Branyrd, and Benedicto too!"

Benedicto bowed his head and turned away so as not to show his emotion. Branyrd smiled when she saw him do this. Even big guys can cry, she thought.

"Well, it's getting late and you all should go to bed. You have a busy day ahead of you getting ready to begin school again now that the sisters have school ready for you," Branyrd announced as she nodded to the sisters.

Sister Superior came over to Branyrd and hugged her and then Benedicto. "Thank you, Angels, for everything you have done to get this island back to life and give the children families to care for them. You have made everyone's lives better."

"It was my mission, Sister, and a pleasure to see everyone happy before we leave. I know you will take care of the children and teach them everything they need to know. I am leaving them in your capable hands."

"We will do our best, Branyrd. After all, we had an exceptional teacher."

The sisters waved goodbye and returned to the orphanage next to the school. They would use the orphanage as their home and needed to settle in and get ready for school the next day.

Benedicto took Branyrd aside and whispered, "It is time for us to leave, Angel. HE has summoned us."

Branyrd looked at the village as all the islanders went back to their homes with the children in tow. She smiled at the sight and wiped her eyes that kept filling up. Branyrd knew that time was different in Heaven from Earth time. By the time she got back to Heaven years would have passed here on Earth. Would they remember her? She hoped they would because she would never forget any of them.

She wiped her tears one last time, smiled at Benedicto and took his arm. "I am ready, Guardian Angel. Let's go."

In a few seconds as the sand swirled around them, they lifted off the beach and headed back to Heaven.

EPILOGUE

Branyrd's head began to clear once she settled onto a cloud in front of HIS domain. HE stood there and waited for her to look up at HIM.

"Well, you are back, Angel. It is a pleasure to see you. I hope you are not upset about leaving again."

"I...I am always disappointed when I have to leave, but I want to come back to YOU, LORD." Branyrd bowed deeper to show her love.

"How do you feel? Do you think that you completed your mission?"

"I...I...think I did, LORD. I did my best." Branyrd did not look up from her bent position. She was not ready to meet

HIS startling eyes in case HE wasn't happy with her performance on her mission.

"Look up at ME, Angel. I promise not to burn you with MY eyes."

Branyrd raised her head and then her eyes to HIM. HE was brighter than she had ever seen HIM but not too bright to her eyes and HE was smiling at her.

"I am pleased with your mission, Branyrd. I couldn't have asked for more from you." Benedicto nodded in agreement and bowed in front of HIM too.

"I am so happy that YOU are pleased with my mission, LORD. What else do YOU want me to do now?"

"Would you like to see how they are doing on Earth on Candle Island of the archipelago?"

"Oh, yes, LORD. Please show me!" Branyrd bowed down and waited for HIS response.

"Stand up, Branyrd and look through this window and you will see for yourself that you have done a commendable job on this mission."

Branyrd stood up as a large window opened in front of her and peered through it. What she saw shocked her. There were people gathered in front of the buildings that she had helped them build and they were building a chapel with a statue of an Angel outside that was carved out of wood. She looked closely and noticed that it looked like her Earthly form. She knew who was responsible for this beautiful carving. She couldn't cry now but could feel her whole body floating and lighter as her wings glistened and fluttered back and forth warming her with the breeze they created.

She sighed and watched as the children passed by the statue and threw it a kiss and bent to say a prayer. The adults did the same thing each time they passed by it and looked up to Heaven as if they could see her. She threw kisses back at them even though she knew they could not see her but would see the rainbows that she spread over them.

She watched the children point upward at the rainbows and smile as they called out to their parents to look up too. The adults blessed themselves and smiled, the sisters bent down and prayed as they looked up to Heaven with tears in their eyes making Branyrd's wings glisten even more.

The village looked like it had grown larger with new buildings since she has been there. A road now led out of the village to the other side of the island where she could see more people were now living in huts there.

Children were playing on the equipment she had left and there were more children than ever before. They all wore happy faces and were tanned and healthy.

Benedicto patted her on her wings and said, "Good job, Angel. They remember you."

"I think they remember you too, Benedicto. Look at the side of the building, there is another statue with a large figure that looks a lot like you!"

"Hmm, so I see. They got the size of my head right. I didn't realize I had such a large head like that with big ears too!" he guffawed.

The LORD slowly closed the window and stepped aside so that the Angels could get one last look before it closed completely.

"Thank you, LORD, for giving me this last glimpse. I hope they will always be as happy as they are now."

"No worries, Angel. I will be watching over them. Rest now and be ready for your next mission."

"When will that be, LORD?" Branyrd asked but the LORD had disappeared.

She smiled and sighed. "Well, I guess I will have to wait until HE is ready to summon me again. Right, Benedicto?"

But her Guardian Angel had done his own disappearing act once again.

THE END

Watch for the next book in the Branyrd the Angel Series coming in 2024!

ABOUT THE AUTHOR

Janice Spina is a retired administrative secretary from a public school system in Massachusetts. She has always loved writing poetry, novels, and children's stories. She published her first book in 2013 and has not stopped since.

This is the 45th book Janice has published. She also has two mystery series of six books each, one for boys and the other for girls even though they are enjoyed by both boys and girls. She has a fantasy series of two books with more to come for YA.

Janice has published 22 children's stories for young children. She also writes under J.E. Spina and has now published eight novels and a short story collection for 18+.

She can be reached at these links.

Website: http://Jemsbooks.com
Blog: https://Jemsbooks.blog
Twitter: http://twitter.com/janice_spina
FB Main Page: http://facebook.com/janice.spina.9
FB Author Page: http://facebook.com/janicespina7
FB Novelist Page: http://facebook.com/jespina7

Janice lives in New Hampshire with her husband, John, and two tanks of fish. John is the illustrator of her children's books and designer of all her book covers.

If you enjoyed this book, please leave a review where you purchased it and spread the word to your family and friends. Janice loves to hear from readers and welcomes reviews from wherever her books are purchased. She says, 'It's like Christmas each time I receive a review!'

If you would like to be on Janice Spina's email list to receive updates, newsletters, and special deals on books, please follow her at her blog/website above.

Watch for more books coming from Jemsbooks.

A NOTE FROM THE AUTHOR

This is the third book in this series about an angel. I infused some comedy into this sometimes-serious story. It deals with many issues that are evident in our world today. I hope you will find it entertaining.

This series is written for young adults – Ages 15+ but younger teens may find it entertaining too. I hope you enjoyed this work of fiction. Watch for another book in this series coming over the next year.

Thank you for purchasing one of Jemsbooks. I appreciate your kind support of me and my books. If you like this book, a review would be greatly appreciated wherever you purchased it. Reviews and word of mouth are the best way to spread your thoughts about books. Please share your review with friends and family. I would love to hear from you. You can reach me at jjspina (at) comcast (dot) net.

All my books are available on Amazon and Barnes & Noble. Watch for more books coming for all ages.

With Blessings & Love,

Janice Spina

OTHER MG/PT/YA BOOKS BY JANICE SPINA for 10+

Davey & Derek Junior Detectives Book 1: The Case of the Missing Cell Phone
  Pinnacle Book Achievement Award,
  Honorable Mention- Readers' Favorite Book Award

Davey & Derek Junior Detectives Book 2: The Case of the Mysterious Black Cat
  Pinnacle Book Achievement Award

Davey & Derek Junior Detectives Book 3: The Case of the Magical Ivory Elephant
  Pinnacle Book Achievement Award
  Reader's Favorite Book Awards – Silver Medal

Davey & Derek Junior Detectives Book 4: The Case of the Brown Scraggly Dog
  Top Shelf Book Awards – First Place
  Finalist in Red Village Review Awards
  5-Star Book Review – Readers' Favorite Book Awards

Davey & Derek Junior Detectives Book 5: The Case of the Sad Mischievous Ghost
 Pinnacle Book Achievement Award & Authorsdb
 Cover Contest – Silver Medal

Davey & Derek Junior Detectives Book 6: The Case of the Mystery of the Bells
 Pinnacle Book Achievement Award
 Finalist – Readers' Favorite Book Awards
 Finalist – Book Excellence Awards

Abby & Holly School Dance
 Pinnacle Book Achievement Award
 Bronze Medal from Readers' Favorite Book Awards

Abby & Holly Series Book 2: Unfortunate Events
 Pinnacle Book Achievement Award
 Readers' Favorite Book Awards – Honorable Mention

Abby & Holly Series, Book 3, Secrets of the Trunk
 Pinnacle Book Achievement Award

Readers' Favorite Book Award 5 Star Review

Abby & Holly Series, Book 4, The Hidden Stairway
Pinnacle Book Achievement Award
Readers' Favorite Book Award 5 Star Review

Abby & Holly Series, Book 5, The Copper Key
Pinnacle Book Achievement Award

Abby & Holly Series, Book 6, Faulty Timeline
Pinnacle Book Achievement Award

YA BOOKS BY JANICE SPINA for 15+

The Legend of the Taken Ones (Gateskin Chronicles Book 1)

5-Star Review from Readers' Favorite Book Awards

Finalist - Book Excellence Awards

The Unknown Territory (Gateskin Chronicles Book 2)

Gateskin Chronicles Book 3 coming in 2024

BOOKS BY J.E. SPINA FOR 17+

The Misunderstood Angel: Branyrd the Angel Series Book 1

Mission of Mercy: Branyrd the Angel Series Book 2

Branyrd the Angel Series Book 4 coming in 2024

BOOKS BY J.E. SPINA FOR 18+

Hunting Mariah

  (Finalist in Authorsdb First Lines Contest)

Mariah's Revenge

  (Finalist in Authorsdb First Lines Contest)

How Far is Heaven

An Angel Among Us: A Short Story Collection

In A Second

Lubelia Alycea: One Hundred Years

www.ingramcontent.com/pod-product-compliance
Lightning Source LLC
Chambersburg PA
CBHW071142260626
47162CB00003B/882